Almost ADULT

PRETEEN STORY DEVOTIONS

CHARLES S. MUELLER

CONCORDIA
PUBLISHING HOUSE

Dedicated to the loving memory of
Martha Magdalene
and
Kurt Horst Claussner
who, in unbelievably trying times,
not only miraculously provided for
their family and kept the Christian
faith, but passed on to their sons a
commitment to both.

Cover Illustration by Ronald R. Hester

Copyright © 1993 Concordia Publishing House
3558 S. Jefferson Avenue, St. Louis, MO 63118-3968
Manufactured in the United States of America

Library of Congress Cataloging-in-Publication Data

Mueller, Charles S.

    Almost adult: preteen story devotions/Charles S. Mueller.

    Summary: As twelve-year-old neighbors Lonnie and Laura move into adulthood, they wrestle with daily problems familiar to everyone. Each of the fifty-nine episodes is accompanied by suggestions for a Scripture passage, an activity, and a prayer thought.

    ISBN 0-570-04598-3

    [1. Christian life—Fiction. 2. Friendship—Fiction.] I. Title.
PZ7.M8784A1   1993
[Fic]—dc20   92-27014

1 2 3 4 5 6 7 8 9 10   02 01 00 99 98 97 96 95 94 93

Contents

Thanksgiving through Christmas

Foreword

Becoming an adult is a complicated matter. Not everyone actually completes the trip. Some get stuck in time, and though their years suggest maturity, their actions deny that reality.

Not everyone who completes the trip does so at the same time in life. Nor in the same way. Whether the actual trip is made, and when, and how well the traveling goes, is related to the will and skill of the travelers, and the support they receive from those with whom God surrounds them. I mean their families. Family is crucial.

What is the specific age of real-life travelers when their crossing takes place? It varies. For some it may happen as early as 9 years of age. For most it is nearer to 12. I believe—and I believe the Bible teaches—that by 12 years of age you are supposed to have completed the journey. From then on you are no longer a child. You are an adult. A *young* adult, mind you. But an adult.

The pages that follow introduce two middle-school students: Laura Meyer and Lonnie Grant. This imaginary twosome, surrounded by a cast of dozens, are in the crossing mode. Watch them. Observe their world. See how they progress and bloom as each, at their own pace, moves along the process of intellectual, physical, spiritual and social development—just like Jesus did at their age (Luke 2:41–52).

I owe a debt of gratitude to the dozens of Almost Adults at Trinity Lutheran Church and School in Roselle, Illinois, who gave me their insight and their ideas. They encouraged me to keep writing about their real world. And I appreciate the steady support of my friend and co-worker, Nelda Piper, whose unflagging effort brought all this to completion.

There's not much else to say. I close wishing all God's children of every age along life's way His blessings. But I reserve a special prayer for His insight upon those who—in this precious moment—are Almost Adult.

Charles S. Mueller

1
Lonnie

Bible Reading: Read Genesis 1:31. What did God see when He "looked out His window"?

When Lonnie Grant looks out his upstairs bedroom window he surveys the world. At least *his* world. And what a world it is!

Down his street toward Second Avenue, Lincoln School juts out. Only his home is more important. Looking the other way he watches the going-ons in back of the Cut-Rate Grocery Store. Between the cracks of the buildings he can look out on Main Street and the cars that whiz by, day or night. Even if he wakes during the night his world speaks to him: Dockum Drug Store's neon sign steadily blinks his way. Toward the north, the flag that flies on a very

9

tall flag pole between the police and fire station waves.

On the Main Street side of Lonnie's house (toward the Cut-Rate) live the Millers. The Millers have no children. Not at home, anyway. The Millers are older. Over 65. But nice. Mr. Miller helped Lonnie find fishing worms last summer.

Behind his house, across the alley, live the Espositos, the Walkers, the Seebers, the Humes, and the Bakers, in that order, from First Avenue to Second, all on Rush Street. The Espositos have a baby, Jamie. The Walkers have a daughter, Rachel, who is six years old.

It's all boys at the Seebers. Three of them. Two are in college and one, Rick, is a senior in high school. The Humes have twins, two years old. Lonnie once watched the twins for Mrs. Humes while she had her hair done. He found out that twins sure are active! Mrs. Humes must have agreed. She gave him five dollars! At the corner lives Mrs. Baker and seven-year-old Lee. Lee's dad doesn't live there. The Bakers are divorced.

East of his house, on Longridge, are two

other houses. At the corner live the Wynns. Michael Wynn helps him with math—and other things. They get along.

Between Lonnie's home and the Wynn's is a very special house. The Meyers live there: Mr. and Mrs. Meyer, Lonnie's good friend (usually, but not always) Laura, and her older sister Kristen. Laura doesn't go to Lincoln School. She attends a Christian school miles away.

There are nights when Lonnie leaves the lights off and slouches down before the window with his chin propped on the sill. In the darkness he looks out at his wonderful world—and feels good!

To Think About: What's your world like? What do you see when you look out your window? Any friends? Name two—and write a word to describe each.

_____

_____

Prayer Thought: Thank God for the things you see out your window.

2
Laura

Bible Reading: Proverbs 18:24 is another helpful word of God. Read it and see if you agree.

Laura Meyer, Lonnie's next-door neighbor, lives in a world similar to his. But not exactly so. For instance, her house is not two-storied like his. Hers is all on one floor, built in a style some call a ranch house. Laura laughed when she first heard her house called that. How could someone residing in a little Illinois town outside Chicago live in a ranch house? No cowpokes or branding irons here!

Laura's bedroom is on the Lincoln-School side of their house, so she can't see Lonnie's big brick home from her bedroom windows. But if she went outside she could. Or if she looked out the family room window she'd see

Lonnie's house, plain as can be. She knows that house almost as well as her own. She's been in it many times. Her family (Mom, Dad, and older sister Kristen) had moved onto Long-ridge Drive almost a year before the Grants.

How do Laura and Lonnie get along? Great! Of course, there are some days they don't talk. And there are even some days they avoid each other. But most days they are friends. That is important because they are the only persons their age in the neighborhood. Laura likes Lonnie. He makes her laugh. She feels he likes her too. Neither says so out loud. If they did, they knew what friends would say and do. Talk about tease!

To Think About: Boys and girls can be friends. It's hard to say that out loud. But it's true. Think of a couple friendly things you might do for a *boy* friend or a *girl* friend. Could you do one of those friendly things tomorrow? If you can, draw a circle around *tomorrow* before you read the next story.

Prayer Thought: Thank Jesus for always claiming you as His friend.

3
Lonnie's Name

Bible Reading: What does Isaiah 43:1 mean to you?

If you don't like your name, join Lonnie's club. He doesn't really like his. It sounds like a girl's name. Or a sissy's.

Actually his name is not Lonnie. It's Alan. That's not much better as far as Lonnie is concerned. His full name is Alan Benjamin Grant, Junior. He was named after his dad, of course. That makes having his name a little better because Lonnie thinks his dad is great. Most of the time.

One day Lonnie told his dad how he felt. As he talked he just blurted out, "Why did you call me Alan?"

"Lonnie," his dad answered, "I was so

proud when you were born! A son! I couldn't think of a better way to tell the world how pleased I was than by giving you my own name. Doing that makes me very careful how I act. I make sure that the name we share is honorable and held in high regard. I do that so *you* will be honored and held in high regard. It works the other way too. I know someday you will bring honor to me by the way you act, and by what you do. People will call me 'Lonnie's dad.' I look forward to it. And when that happens, I hope you'll feel better about 'our' name."

Actually Lonnie didn't have to wait for the good feelings to start growing. He started feeling better as soon as his dad told him how he felt. His name now meant something special to him. It meant he was the much-loved son of a proud father.

To Think About: Do you like your name? Can you think of another name you'd like better? Write it here: _____. Why that name? _____
What does the name *Christian* mean to you?

Prayer Thought: Thank God for giving you the name *Christian*.

15

4
Laura's First Name: Baby X

Bible Reading: Jesus was given a special name for a special reason. Read Matthew 1:18–21. What does Jesus' name mean?

Talk about interesting stories! Would you believe Laura had no name for the first three days of her life? She was just "Baby X." But I'm getting ahead of myself. Let me start at the beginning.

When Laura was born, her parents couldn't come up with an acceptable name. Neither could think of a name both really liked. The nurses at the hospital kept bugging Mrs. Meyers about a name for the birth certificate. They could come up with nothing. Dawn? No. Lillian? No. Grace? Sandy? Kate? No. No. No.

It was at that point Pastor Hinz came to the rescue.

When he visited Mrs. Meyer at the hospital, she told him of their troublesome indecision. His solution? Check the family tree. Both sides. The first name *that is the same on both sides* should be the baby's name!

"In moments of doubt trust your ancestors' wisdom," the pastor said.

That's what Mr. and Mrs. Meyers did. They dug out both family trees and started comparing names. Would you believe it? Two great-great grandmothers (one on each side) had first names that matched: Laura. What a coincidence! But more. Great-Great-Grandmother Laura Huff *died on the same day in 1943 as baby Laura was born many years later* and Great-Great Grandmother Laura Williams *was born on the same date in 1874 as Baby X!* Incredible? That being true, what else could they name her but Laura?

And so it was: Laura Marie Meyer was officially named three days after her birth. The nurses were glad. Pastor Hinz liked it too. One more coincidence—Laura was his mother's name.

To Think About: Laura was named on January 6. On what date was she born? Do you know the significance of that date? Think about it. I'll give you a hint: EP__P__A__Y. If you still don't know the answer look at the end of story 7. Now a bigger job: Find someone to tell you, or help you discover, what that word means and write your answer here:

_____

_____

Prayer Thought: Tell God your favorite name for Him and explain why you like it best.

5
The Home Where Laura Lives

Bible Reading: Read Psalm 23. Do you think the psalm applies to your home life?

The Meyers lived longer on Longridge than the Grants. The day the Grants moved in Laura took a box of cookies over to their house. She was barely three. Lonnie watched her from his hiding place behind his mother's knee. He didn't say a word.

Laura and her family are members of Christ Church. Laura has attended Christ Day School since kindergarten. Christ Day School is four miles away. That means getting up a little earlier every school day than Lonnie. Sometimes as she slides into the back seat of the car, ready for the ride to school, she sees Lonnie in his kitchen eating breakfast. He walks barely three blocks to school. She tried to explain to him why she goes so far. He didn't understand. How could he? He didn't think of school as a place to learn more about Jesus!

Laura's dad and mom both work. Her mom is a pharmacist at Dockum Drugs on Main. Mr. Meyer sells tires at Big Joe's Tire Works. He thinks that is a dumb name for a place that is one of the leading tire stores in Illinois. But it doesn't stop people from buying there.

Kristen, Laura's older sister, can be loads of fun one day and a total pain the next. She grouches when she thinks Laura is listening to her telephone conversations with the boys that call. She also complains that Laura might use one of her tapes. Or mess up her makeup. Actually Laura doesn't care about Kristen's things. She doesn't even go into Kristen's room when no one is home! Well, not most of the time.

Until July 4 each year, when Lonnie has

his birthday, Laura is one year older than he is, and lords it over him. Just a little. Lately, something is changing in her feelings toward Lonnie. She's always felt he was a friend. Now she's aware that he is a *boy* friend. Nothing serious, mind you. She just has low-level awareness.

To Think About: How do you and your brother/sister get along? If you don't have one, how well do your friends get along with theirs? Think about it and circle a number from 1 (bad) to 10 (super).

1 2 3 4 5 6 7 8 9 10

What might be done to improve your evaluation?

Prayer Thought: Ask God for the special help you need in getting along with a brother, sister, or friend.

6
Life at Lonnie's

Bible Reading: Read Leviticus 19:18. Part of that verse is repeated time and again in Scripture. Could it be saying that before you will love your neighbor, you must love yourself? What do you think?

We've made a quick hike around the block and taken a look at the residents of every house, except one. We haven't looked in at 260 Longridge where Lonnie, his mom and dad, his older sister Betty, and little brother Steven all live. And Rocket, their dog.

You will like Lonnie. He's a nice guy. You'll like his sister and brother too. Betty is 16 and a lot kinder to Lonnie than Laura's sister Kristen is to her. Little brother Steve is no bother. Lonnie can spend a whole evening playing a game with him or running the trains they "own" together.

But not everything is super about the Grant home. For one thing, they don't attend church. Laura is on Lonnie's back a lot about that. Mr. and Mrs. Grant aren't against Jesus or church. They just haven't been stirred to action.

Lonnie has been thinking. Something inside him keeps telling him to take up Laura on her invitation to join her family at Christ Church some Sunday morning. One of the things that makes Lonnie wonder about church is a growing awareness that he's not the smartest kid in the world. He *knows* he's not the smartest kid in class. The tutoring he needed from Michael Wynn in order to pass math convinced him of that. He doesn't read as fast as some, or think as quickly in some subjects, or get the point of a lesson as swiftly as many others. But when it comes to athletics and getting along with people, he's tops. Lonnie wonders whether there might be something wrong with him. Some learning disability, maybe?

What makes him think of that? He overheard a conversation between his mom and dad. They were concerned about how long it took him to do things at school. After overhearing their concern, Lonnie wondered whether maybe the reason Laura was so much quicker than he was because she went to church. Possible? You never know, he thought to himself.

To Think About: Lonnie is not sure just who he really is, or what his gifts are. Do you think all people understand themselves? Do you think Jesus loves you, whoever you are?

Prayer Thought: Thank Jesus for thinking you're special enough to die for.

7
Lonnie's Parents

Bible Reading: Read Exodus 20:12. Many call this verse the _____ Commandment.

You already know Lonnie's dad's name. Alan Benjamin Grant. He's also called Senior. Alan Benjamin Grant, Senior. If you want the whole thing, it's Officer Alan Benjamin Grant, Senior. He is a policeman. A good one too.

Lonnie's mom? She tells people she's "just a housewife." That makes Mr. Grant sputter. He tried to change her attitude by hanging a sign in the kitchen. It said, "The woman of the house is a professional—a household engineer."

Lonnie isn't the only one that thinks about church. Gerry (Lonnie's mom) and Alan Senior think and talk about it too. They feel like something is missing in their life. Both agree it is probably church.

The Meyers have invited them to join them in worship, but they came as spectators, not participants. Now things are beginning to bother them—their own sense of need, Lonnie's grades, Betty's preparing for college, and Steven's questions about God and heaven.

Something else is making them think—a conversation they overheard between Laura and Lonnie. The two of them were talking in the driveway outside the kitchen window and their words drifted in. Laura was telling Lonnie that her teacher at school said children grow up acting like their father and thinking like their mother. Alan looked at Gerry. Could that be true?

To Think About: The word *honor* can mean *to weigh*. What could it mean that God wants you to *weigh* your parents' actions and attitudes? By the way, the answer to the question in story 4 is *EPIPHANY*.

Prayer Thought: Ask God to help you carefully weigh your parents' words and actions.

8
Lincoln School

Bible Reading: You'll like Proverbs 22:6. If you "train up a child" what happens when the child gets old? _____

Lincoln School is only two-and-a-half blocks from Lonnie's house. Close. On a nice day he can run to school in less than three minutes. Rainy days are different. Then the school seems many soggy miles away. Lonnie has attended Lincoln since kindergarten. That's a long time! Now he can almost see the end of his Lincoln School days. Yep. Next year Lonnie will leave Lincoln and head off to Whitmore Middle School, down on Main Street, five blocks beyond the hospital. If he passes! He's going to walk there too. Whitmore is further away than Lincoln, but it's still too close for the school bus pick up.

Lonnie's teacher at Lincoln is Amy Ruther. *Mrs.* Amy Ruther. She's nice. And does she ever control the class! No one gets rowdy when she's in charge. Yet when it's time for fun she's right there!

What's school like at Lincoln? The same every day. First a warning bell rings, then follows an organized explosion of students trying to squeeze down the hall to the right room in order to settle into the right chair at the right desk before the second bell rings. Then Mrs. Ruther checks attendance and sends Jim Bow to the office with the attendance slip. As soon as Jim gets back, she makes announcements, then everybody stands, faces the flag, puts their hand over their heart, and says the Pledge of Allegiance.

From there on the tempo picks up. Things blur. Open your books. Close your books. Sign your name. Fill in the blanks. Underline the word. Take out your math. Time for recess. With Mrs. Ruther in charge, six hours of class zip to the last actions of the day: clean off your desk, straighten your chair, wait for the bell, you are dismissed.

Whew! No breaks from start to finish! If it isn't Mrs. Ruther pushing and teaching, its other kids with stories to tell, cards to trade, jokes to share, and games to play. Who says school is easy? Or dull!

To Think About: What's your school day like? Why not keep a diary for one day? When you have done so, put a star beside what was most fun, an exclamation point beside what was hardest to do, an asterisk by what you do best. And how about a cross next to everything you feel is God's gift to you?

Prayer Thought: Think through your school day. Thank God for the good things and ask His help with things that trouble you.

9
Christ Day School

Bible Reading: Try reading Daniel 1:1–8. Every time you come to a name hard to read, either sound it out or skip it. The story is about some of God's children growing up in a non-Christian school.

While Lonnie often sees Laura leave for school, she never sees Lonnie leave—except when she's home sick or when their vacation days don't quite match. Laura's school is Christ Day School, nearly four miles away. She's in the same grade as Lonnie and uses many of the same books, but there are differences. Real ones too! Like the way the school day begins.

There's the same kind of bell. And the same kind of hurrying to get to the right seat.

And, yes, Mr. Rolf takes attendance too. Then comes the same Pledge of Allegiance. After that things get different. How?

First, Mr. Rolf asks if anyone has a prayer request. Now that's different! Usually one or more suggests a prayer about something in the news—a flood, a fire, or a tragedy. Then Mr. Rolf might write the name of a missionary on the board. He tells the class how that missionary shares the love of Jesus in some faraway place. With all that in place the class has its prayer, usually led by Mr. Rolf. Sometimes Pastor Hinz stops by and leads the prayer.

After the prayer the part of the day Laura likes best takes place: religion class. Some days the students study a Bible story. Sometimes they study with a workbook and discuss topics. Other days they might watch a video, slides, or a movie. Why does Laura like religion class so much? Two reasons: She likes hearing about what God has done and is still doing in the world, and it makes her think.

After religion class things at Christ Day School are very much like things at Lincoln School. But all day Laura is surrounded by reminders of Jesus. She sees crosses, pictures, Christian symbols. And more. At her school they don't talk religion all the time, but Laura feels Jesus' warming presence every day and in many ways. Especially when Mr. Rolf deals with a class problem. Especially then.

To Think About: In what ways does your Sunday or day school teacher help you learn about God? Do you ever share your faith with your teacher? How?

Prayer Thought: Ask God to help you share your faith at school.

10
Mr. Rolf

Bible Reading: Philippians 2:5–9 shows us how Christ took our place. Read the words slowly and underline three or four words which describe what Jesus did.

Mr. Rolf is very special to Laura. He is a good teacher and knows how to be a friend to the class. Most of the kids had never had a man teacher before. At first they were a little afraid of him. It wasn't until *it* happened that the class realized Mr. Rolf was someone very special.

It happened like this.

Ron Burton sometimes said bad words. Everyone had heard those words before but, as Mrs. Carter, their third grade teacher, had explained, "Certain words have meanings which upset our nature and disturb the way we relate with each other. We don't use them."

Maybe *we* don't, but Ron did. On the sly. When he thought no adult would hear. One day an adult did hear: Mr. Rolf. At recess, Ron exploded his favorite string of not-very-nice words. When he turned around with a grin on his face, there was Mr. Rolf. Right behind him. Good-bye grin!

The kids who saw it all happen told Laura the rest. They said Mr. Rolf didn't shout, didn't threaten, and didn't grab. Instead he walked up to Ron, put his hand on his shoulder, and called those who had heard Ron's words to come and stand by the two of them.

"Ron," he said, "I'm sorry I heard you say those words. And judging from the look on your face, you're sorry too. Right?"

Ron ducked his head and nodded.

"You're not the first person who has used that kind of language, nor, I'm sure, the last. But I'd like this to be the last time that language is used *here*. Wouldn't it be great if you could just take a deep breath and pull all those words back into your mouth? I wish that were possible. But it's not. However, we *can* do something to remind ourselves about being careful with our speech."

Mr. Rolf continued, "How about if, after school, you and I get a bucket of water, some soap, and a brush. Together, let's clean about ten concrete blocks in the hall—the ones by the drinking fountain that are always so dirty because students wipe their hands against them all day long. We'll clean five blocks each and let those clean blocks remind us that we can keep our language clean. We'll clean the dirt the same way Jesus cleaned our dirt—our sin— by washing it away."

Mr. Rolf and Ron scrubbed ten blocks that afternoon. Together. In the process they did more than clean a wall. They became friends. And the class saw how a Christian teacher acts. Ron was much more careful about his language after that.

To Think About: Do you think Mr. Rolf did the right thing the right way? How do his actions make you think of Christ's?

Prayer Thought: Thank God for the teachers who show you Jesus.

11
Lonnie Takes a Test

Bible Reading: Matthew 14:22–33 is about a test. Did anyone pass?

The voice of doom! No real warning. And now no way to avoid it. Mrs. Ruther's announcement hit Lonnie like a truck: Math test next Tuesday.

Tuesday! *Next* Tuesday? How could he be ready by Tuesday? Things were just now getting better. He hadn't told Mrs. Ruther he was being tutored by Michael Wynn. He didn't know how she'd take it. Lonnie didn't feel like he was ready for a test! But he couldn't ask for more help from Michael, Michael had a school dance this weekend. Actually Lonnie didn't think his brain could stand any more of Michael's pushing.

Of course Lonnie *could* study on his own. But not for a test! Still, Michael had said he was doing great. And Mrs. Ruther's comment after his last homework was, "Why, Lonnie, this looks just fine!" But what did that mean? Nothing now. Tuesday was dooms day! For sure. That's how Lonnie thought and felt as he walked home Friday afternoon.

Lonnie's attitude hadn't improved by Saturday. But he did page around in his math book for half an hour. By Sunday he was desperate. He put in another hopeless period of study. Monday dragged on like a day with 60 hours. As Mrs. Ruther reviewed things for Tuesday's test, Lonnie tried to absorb every word she said.

Tuesday dawned. The test came down his aisle, passed from student to student, as if it were a rattlesnake slithering its way to strike him with poisonous fangs. Lonnie took one paper and passed the rest over his shoulder to Noreen who sat right behind him. He signed his name, taking as much time as he could, dawdling until there was no more escape. Finally, he had to start. He had to begin.

Hey! Wait a minute here! He knew the answer to number 1. And some of number 2 too. He knew numbers 3, 5, 6, and 8. Number 4 was a mystery. Numbers 9 and 10 looked familiar enough for a good guess. What a surprise! That's the way the test went.

On Wednesday Lonnie got the results: 82%. Not bad, though he could never figure out how you could take a test with 10 questions and get 82%. And he also began to wonder whether, between Michael's tutoring and his studying, he just might pass math—and maybe even get a B!

To Think About: Do you think people are always as powerless as they often feel when faced with something they fear? Write the first initial of what you fear here: _____ God helps us face fear. Isn't that what Psalm 46:1 says?

_____ Yes
_____ No

Prayer Thought: Tell God about something that you fear.

12
The Cheater

Bible Reading: There is a story about cheating in Acts 5:1–6. Scary, right? What do you think about it?

The first time Laura saw it happen, it almost took her breath away. That was in the second grade. Laura saw Beth cheat. The class was taking a spelling test. Laura saw Beth look over to Tom's paper, cock her head so she could see clearly, and copy his answer. Laura saw that, but she did nothing. She liked Beth. They were friends.

As the years passed, Laura realized Beth had kept on cheating. She would copy homework from Leon and peek at Sue Ann's multiple choice test. Once she traced Audrey's map of Indiana, even though the teacher had said each was to draw one.

The straw that broke the camel's back happened last week. On a true/false test in which the minus sign was the mark for false and the plus sign was the sign for true, Beth put a minus for every answer. Then when the teacher went over the answers after the test, but before they were turned in, Beth casually made all the minus signs pluses on the questions that should be answered true. She got a 100 on the test and a word of praise from Mr. Rolf. That was too much. Laura had had enough. It was time for action. But what was she to do?

First Laura thought and prayed about it. Then she decided to talk to Beth. It wasn't easy. It wasn't pleasant telling Beth that she had been watching her cheat for years. She told Beth that cheating was wrong. And Beth? What did she say? She said, *So?* Just like that! *So?*

That upset Laura. Without thinking she said, "So, this. If I see you cheat one more time, I'm going to stand up in class and say out loud, 'Mr. Rolf, Beth is cheating again.' That's what I'm going to do."

Beth blinked. She looked carefully at Laura. She didn't say anything more. But she stopped cheating. At least she stopped cheating when Laura was watching. Their relationship cooled. Laura didn't let that bother her. She felt she had done what was right for Beth and for the rest of the school.

To Think About: Do you think Laura did the right thing? What else might she have done? Even if you think Laura's actions were okay, could she have said something different to Beth that wouldn't have sounded so tough?

Prayer Thought: Ask God to help you stand up for your faith in ways that share His love.

13
Everyone Likes Lonnie

Bible Reading: 1 Samuel 18:14–16 tells us about what a great guy _____ was.

Everyone likes Lonnie. His classmates like him. Adults like him. Teachers, neighbors, and even little children like him.

Maybe that's why Lonnie is usually selected to be the captain, or president, or leader. He may not get the best grades, but he knows how to deal with people and is especially good at giving everyone in his group a chance to shine. Likeable Lonnie.

Athletics? Lonnie does okay. Others hit the ball harder, and kick more goals, and make more free throws, but he's almost always chosen first. Why? He knows how to make a team work. Likeable Lonnie.

His teachers say that Lonnie is a natural leader, whatever *that* means. Lonnie just tries to give everyone a chance and help kids work as a team.

Bill, his good buddy since third grade, has noticed something else about Lonnie. Lonnie never says negative thing about others. Not even about his teachers. When Bill mentioned this to Lonnie in front of some other kids, Lonnie just laughed. The other kids nodded in agreement, teased him a little, and wondered to themselves why he was like that.

To Think About: A lot of what St. Paul says about Christian conduct is just common sense—applied. Read 1 Corinthians 13, especially verses 4–6. Underline the words which, when applied, will make almost anyone likeable. How does Jesus' love make you likeable?

Prayer Thought: Ask God to help you share the kind of love St. Paul describes.

14

But Laura Is Different

Bible Reading: Psalm 86:7 tells us we can call on _____ when we have problems. What kind of *people* problems do you have?

"Laura, you have to keep more of your opinions to yourself. People don't like your blunt honesty. Besides, keeping track of people who cheat in your class is none of your business. That's your teacher's job. Just take care of yourself. No one put you in charge of the school!"

Whew! Laura was shocked by her mother's reaction to her story about Beth's cheating and what she had done. She had expected words of encouragement and approval. Instead she got a lecture.

When Laura saw Lonnie in his backyard, she told him about it. Lonnie listened. Mrs. Meyer's reaction surprised him too. He didn't try to understand it. About all he could do was offer his opinion and give a slightly different twist to what took place.

"Laura," he said, "your talk with Beth took lots of courage. I don't know if I could have done it. But I don't know if you ought to really stand up and report her in class. She'd probably hate you the rest of her life! Watch and see what happens. Then maybe you'll find another way to deal with it. Or, maybe she'll change!"

Laura felt better after talking to Lonnie. She often did. For someone who had trouble with math and reading, he sure made sense. He was a good friend too.

From the kitchen window Mrs. Meyer watched them talk. Actually she *was* proud of Laura. But she worried about her too. Laura was smart and grown-up for her age. Yet she seemed to have trouble getting along with others. Some days Mrs. Meyer wished she wasn't as mature in some ways and as uncontrolled in others. Or maybe she wished that these difficult years for Laura would hurry along a little faster. When would Laura learn more about making and keeping friends? A thought struck her: Was there some way Lonnie could teach Laura his friendship skills! And deeper in her mind a second fleeting thought: Maybe Laura could help Lonnie, and his parents, get to know more about Jesus. Maybe.

To Think About: Think about making and keeping friends. Write down a couple of things that people who make friends seem to do well:

_____

_____

_____

Prayer Thought: Ask God's help in knowing how to talk to friends.

15
Lonnie's Teacher Isn't Fair

Bible Reading: People aren't always fair. But God is. Agree? How does Micah 7:18 help you see that?

Lonnie likes Mrs. Ruther. He also feels Mrs. Ruther likes him. Of course, she doesn't like him as much as she likes Naomi Pauley or Ted Westermann. They are special to her. But still she likes him. Any wonder Lonnie was surprised when she wasn't fair to the class, to his spelling team, or to him? It happened like this.

Mrs. Ruther wanted the students to improve their spelling skills. She divided the class into five teams. Lonnie was chosen captain of one of the teams, even though he isn't the best speller. Juanita Lopez is the best speller.

But back to Mrs. Ruther. She told the class that the five teams would compete against each other in spelling bees for four weeks. At the end of four weeks whichever team had won the most often could plan a Friday last-hour party—and do whatever they wanted. Within reason, of course.

The first week Lonnie's team won. Why not? Juanita was on his side. But the second week Mildred Orson's team won. The third week Chuck Black's team won. It looked like there would be no clear winner. But the fourth week Lonnie's team really started cooking! Juanita coached them, especially Lonnie. The competition came down, on the last day, to Lonnie and the word *signify*. He got the *s*, the *i*, the *g*, and the *n* easily. But the next letter! In his mind he wondered whether it should be an *a*, an *e*, an *i*, or maybe a *u*. *O* was out. He took a deep breath and said it: *i-f-y*. Juanita clapped first. Then the team joined in. They had won! The Friday last-hour party choice was theirs.

Lonnie's team told Mrs. Ruther that they wanted to bring Nintendos and TV sets. For the last hour Friday they would have a Nintendo Contest.

Mrs. Ruther said no. She added something about it being too complicated and dangerous. Something might get broken. And the school had no insurance.

As far as Lonnie and the class were concerned, Mrs. Ruther broke her word. She wasn't fair.

To Think About: Do you think Mrs. Ruther broke her word? _____ Supposing she did, how ought people of God react to broken promises? Aren't you glad God doesn't break His?

Prayer Thought: Thank God for keeping His promises.

16
Laura Gets a Demerit

Bible Reading: Lamentations 3:31–33 tells us that God isn't trying to find ways to punish us. 1 Timothy 2:3–4 tells us what He wants to do. God wants to _____ everybody.

It was so embarrassing. It wouldn't be to some kids, but it was to Laura. She got a demerit. No, that's not quite the right way to say what happened. She had been "looking for" a demerit for about a week, and today she found it. Or it found her. Whatever. Until today, each time something improper happened, Mr. Rolf would let it pass. This time he gave her the demerit.

At Christ Day School students get demerits when they talk in class, or come unprepared, or arrive late in the morning. Things like that. Larry Stone talked back to Mr. Rolf. *Three* demerits! All at once. And Marion Rogers refused to pick up some papers in the hall when the principal asked. She told him she hadn't dropped them and that she wasn't the janitor. Four demerits.

If a student gets 10 demerits, a note is sent home. If a student gets 15, the parents and student must meet with the teacher. Students who get 25 demerits may be expelled.

Do you know how many demerits Laura had received so far this year? Zero. Same last year. As a matter of fact she had never received a demerit in all her years at Christ. But lately Laura had been walking on the demerit-edge.

When class began yesterday, Mr. Rolf had to say, "Laura, we're ready to begin. Please stop talking." After the morning recess he said, "Laura, the bell has rung. It's time to return to your seat." At noon he said, "Laura, I don't believe you cleaned up where you were eating." Then, at 1:34 P.M., he said, "Laura, that will be one demerit. I asked you to open your science book, not your library book. In the future please do what you are told."

Getting a demerit is no big deal to most kids. But to Laura it was devastating. It became a life-long warning that just because you are smart doesn't mean you are above the rules.

Laura got over the demerit. But she never forgot the lesson. In some ways it was one of the best things that ever happened to her.

To Think About: I get the feeling Laura got her demerit because she was testing Mr. Rolf. Do people do that? Sure. They even "test" God. See if you can think of a story from the Bible— or from life—in which people tested God.

Prayer Thought: Thank God for loving you, even when you test Him.

17
Laura's Report Card

Bible Reading: If we try to pass heaven's entry exam without Jesus at our side, Romans 3:23 tells us what our grade will be: _____.

I don't want you to feel that Laura is too good to be true. She's smart, but she also works hard at her studies. She does her assignments and gets them in on time. She spends at least an hour every day on her homework. Saturday and Sunday too. So it's no surprise that she gets good grades and that teachers like her. Laura's report card is a page of *A's.*

Laura's parents are careful about what they say about grades. Kristen does not do as well in school as Laura. They are afraid that if they say too much Kristen might get discouraged or Laura might get a big head and quit studying. You know how parents are!

How does Lonnie feel about Laura's report cards? He is impressed. He has never felt inferior to Laura. He figures that if he can run faster than she can, and hit a ball harder, what difference does it make if she gets better grades?

And Laura. She likes books and new knowledge, so she just keeps going. She studies. But lately she is careful to whom she shows her report card. It is obvious to her that not everyone is glad about her good grades. Not like Lonnie is. He says things like *Wow!* or *Look at that!* She knows he is saying how happy he is for her. For the last year or so, one of the best things about getting good grades has been showing them to Lonnie.

To Think About: What's the value of grades anyway? Circle as many of the following as you think apply: They encourage hard work. They rate the teacher. They show progress. They prove how good you are.

Prayer Thought: Ask God for help in improving some study habits.

18
Making the Team

Bible Reading: I think St. Paul would have enjoyed our modern Olympics. Read 2 Timothy 4:7–8 and see if you agree. The *crown* mentioned is the leafy halo Greeks gave athletes who came in first! What are two events Paul wouldn't have missed?

_____

_____

Is there any time in the year more tense than the day or two just before the coach tacks to the bulletin board the names of those who made the basketball team? Or when Mrs. Homp publishes this year's cheerleading squad? Talk about tension! Kids are nervous as a cat on those days. But Lonnie isn't.

Lonnie never worries about making any

team. He always makes it. He is good enough at any game that there is no question he will make the team. He starts each game too. Lonnie isn't big, but he is quick. In games like basketball he has a sense of the floor and knows where to pass the ball. He loves to pass to the open man. That's another reason he always makes the team: He is a team player. Lonnie likes to score, and does. But he also likes it when others score. The coaches like that quality. So do the other players.

The only thing that bothers Lonnie about teams is being confused about what he can say to some of his friends who don't make it. Do you tell them they have limited skill, or that they don't understand the game, or that they don't hit the open man? He especially worries about Mark.

Mark isn't going to make the team. Even though Mark doesn't realize this, Lonnie does. Why won't Mark make it? Take your choice. Mark can't shoot. He gets confused in the game. He is more likely to fire up a brick from long distance than pass to a teammate. No, Mark won't make it. But Lonnie likes Mark. His liking Mark makes these announcement days tough.

Lonnie has explained all this to Mark. Mark *uh-huhs* him. But when the team is posted, Mark always sings the same song: The coach has it in for me. Lonnie knows Mark is about to go through the same routine again. He wishes Mark would change. Or that he could think up something new and helpful to say to Mark.

Uh-oh! They're all bunched around the bulletin board. There's Mark. He's reading the list. He's turning away. He's upset.

What am I going to say to him this time? wonders Lonnie as he walks toward Mark.

To Think About: If Lonnie knows how Mark will feel and he doesn't know what to say, why doesn't Lonnie just avoid Mark for a while? What's your answer? Mine is at the end of the next story.

Prayer Thought: Thank God for keeping you on His team.

19
The Substitute Teacher

Bible Reading: In Exodus 4:1 Moses worries he won't be accepted as the leader. Could his fears be those of any leader—like a teacher?

Mr. Rolf doesn't miss class often. He is seldom sick. But today he has to attend a conference on teaching computer skills. So who is to teach in his place? Miss Lurvey, the substitute. That can mean trouble. A lot of kids see a substitute teacher as their chance to goof off and get away with almost anything. What do they care about Miss Lurvey? If she reports them to Mr. Rolf, they can always say they didn't understand what she meant.

But for Laura, dealing with a substitute teacher isn't that simple. She is pretty sure that

Mr. Rolf will tell the substitute teacher that she can answer any questions about what had been assigned or what they have discussed. Ask Laura. She'll know.

Laura *does* know. She pays attention. She also knows that if she tells Miss Lurvey the truth, the kids will give her a hard time.

Here's what happened.

The morning went well. Miss Lurvey got some discussion going about the eating habits of the Plains Indians and Jesus' feeding of the 5000! Noon came. And lunch. And 20 fast minutes outside. It was just enough time for an argument to start over a kick ball game. When the kids came back inside—hot, sweaty, and irritated—their mood of cooperation had vanished. Miss Lurvey was in trouble.

"Spelling test," said Miss Lurvey.

"Not today," interrupted Myron. "We don't have spelling tests on Tuesdays."

A lot of kids nodded in agreement and murmured their support. Then the bomb dropped.

Looking her way, Miss Lurvey asked, "Is that correct, Laura?"

Laura wanted to sink through the floor. She knew the truth: Tuesday was spelling day. She also knew what would be safest to say. What should she do—especially in a Christian school? What would *you* do?

To Think About: Laura had some choices. She could say, "I'm not sure, Miss Lurvey." "I believe Myron is right." "Sometimes Mr. Rolf skips tests on Tuesdays." "We are to have a test this Tuesday." Any other answers come to mind? Write one down.

(Here's my answer to the last story's question: Because they were friends, and Lonnie hadn't yet learned that a true friend is a great person to trust with the truth, especially the truth about something important.)

Prayer Thought: Thank God for helping you out in a tough situation.

20
A Visit to the Principal's Office

Bible Reading: Read Luke 10:30–37. What's the point Jesus makes?

_____

_____

It hadn't been a good week for Lonnie. On Monday he lost his homework. Really. He tried to explain it to Mrs. Ruther. She didn't buy his story. On Tuesday he ran into a parked car with his bike. It didn't do much damage to the car, but it bent his front wheel and scared him. What a shock! He still couldn't figure out how that happened. Wednesday had been the thing with Mark and the basketball team. *That* was no fun at all! Now here he was on Thursday reluctantly marching down the hall to the principal's office. Why? Because he had tried to rescue Lee Baker's cat. It happened like this.

Lonnie had gotten up plenty early that Thursday so he would have no problem eating his cereal with bananas and getting to school on time. Last week he had cut it too close twice and got to class just a little late. Mrs. Ruther's response to his excuse was, "One more tardy and you'll have to talk to the principal."

No problem, he thought to himself. I'll just be a little more careful. Then the cat thing happened.

As he was leaving his house for school (in plenty of time), he saw Lee Baker trying to climb the big elm by his house. He wasn't doing a very good job of it. And it sounded like he was crying. So Lonnie strolled over to see what was going on. There on the first big limb was Lee's cat, meowing away. That cat had gotten up into the tree, but it couldn't get down! What to do? Without thinking, Lonnie dropped his books, shinnied up the tree, grabbed the cat, slipped down the tree and turned the pet over to Lee. It all took two minutes. He still had plenty of time.

Now the problem. Coming down the tree Lonnie had split the rear seam of his pants. He could feel air. What else could he do but run back home, change pants, and then make the mad dash to school? And guess what. Tardy! Again.

He'd tried to explain what had happened to Mrs. Ruther. He wasn't sure whether she believed him or not. She listened, gave him an odd smile, but still sent him to the principal.

"A rule's a rule," Mrs. Ruther said as she patted him on the shoulder. Now he had to explain it all to the principal who didn't often smile.

A guy tries to do something nice and what happens! He gets into trouble. It's not fair!

To Think About: Jesus came to help us. Circle *T* for *true* or *F* for *false*. It didn't cost Him anything. *T F*. We didn't need His help. *T F*. Check your answers to those two statements against Romans 5:6–10.

Prayer Thought: Thank Jesus for paying the price to save you.

21
The Play—
Part 1

Bible Reading: 2 Corinthians 13:11 says many good things about the way those who love Jesus live. One is that Christians should live in ____ with one another. Is that easy? possible? What do you think?

It wasn't just the musical's title that caught Laura's eye. It was the announcement that tryouts for this year's school play, *Welcome to England,* were to be held. She thought that title was dumb. The description made things sound a little better: "An American girl visits English relatives for the summer and decides to stay for a year. Hilarious escapades. Great songs. Some dance. For a cast of six males and nine females." It still didn't sound *that* great. But it was their school play, the only one this year.

Laura read on: "Tryouts for Mary, the American girl, will be held at 3:00 P.M. Wednesday. Sign below." She looked at the sign-up sheet. One name. *The* name. Karen Richards.

Karen Richards was always the lead in their class plays. As long as Laura could remember! Karen could sing. She could act. She could even dance a little. But she wasn't the only girl in the class! Others could be the lead too! If they only had a chance!

Laura reached out, took the pencil hanging on the string next to the announcement, and signed her name: Laura Meyer.

Hardly had she finished when she changed her mind. What had she done? Could she erase it? No way. Anyone could still see her name. Why did she sign? She'd never be able to compete with Karen! But it was too late.

"Go for it, Laura," said Lonnie when she told him about it that afternoon. "You can do it! The worst thing that can happen is that Karen will win again."

No, thought Laura, that's not the worst thing that could happen. The worst thing that could happen would be embarrassing myself in front of the whole class. Why did I ever do it? Why did I ever sign my name?

To Think About: Does a Christian compete against another Christian? And what do you do when you are not only competing against someone else, but against your own self-esteem too?

Prayer Thought: Ask Jesus to help you remember that you can do all things through Him.

22
The Play—Part 2

Bible Reading: Does Hebrews 13:1 make sense to you? It sounds like it's telling us to keep on loving one another. That's tough, right? But with God's help it just might be possible. What do you think?

Laura's palms were sweating. Her tummy was tumbling. Her knees were knocking. Her voice quivered. She gulped a lot. At first. But as she got into the song, all that went away.

Mr. Norem, the director, was playing the piano. His assistant, Mrs. Murray, stood in front of Laura, smiling and nodding. Tryouts for *Welcome to England* were moving right along. Laura had read a few lines, danced a few steps, and was now singing. The reading wasn't bad. The dancing was not so hot. The singing had started out weak. But it got better. She sang the theme song of the play, a nice melody that was easy to learn. She almost enjoyed herself.

"Very nice," said Mrs. Murray when Laura finished. "You have such a pleasing voice. And it's so full! Where have you been hiding? We'll post the results tomorrow after Mr. Norem and I have had a chance to consult."

The next day the cast list was stapled to the bulletin board. You guessed it: Karen Richards got the part of Mary. Laura was chosen too. Her role was Vivian, Mary's English friend. But it was a very small part. Oh, one more thing: Laura was also chosen as the understudy for Karen!

And one more thing. Mrs. Murray stopped Laura in the hall and said, "You really surprised me yesterday, Laura. I was pleased you tried out. That took a lot of courage and shows character. And I was delighted with your voice. It's not quite as full as Karen's. But I think that with time and training you can be a very good singer. If you don't mind, I'd like to talk with your mother about that."

Laura nodded her yes, turned around, and floated down the hall. *Me?* A good singer? she asked herself.

After that experience some kids in her class seemed warmer toward her, especially Karen Richards. Could it be that Laura was making friends? Just by signing up for a tryout?

No question about it.

To Think About: Laura was a "winner" in life because she tried out. You can be a life-winner too. But you do have to "try." Becoming an eternal-life winner is different. Ephesians 2:8–9 will tell you about that.

Prayer Thought: Thank Jesus for doing the work to win you eternal life.

23
The Thief

Bible Reading: Deuteronomy 5:19 tells us we should not _____. Why is that subject worth a commandment?

Ray was angry as he said, "Okay, Lonnie. Give it back. It was there when I left. You were the last one in the locker room. Now it's gone. Give it back."

Lonnie couldn't believe his ears. Was this his friend Ray accusing him, practically nose to nose! They had played ball together since third grade. He'd gone to every one of Ray's birthday parties. And Ray had come to his. Now Ray was accusing him of stealing a wallet with seven bucks in it.

At first Lonnie tried to laugh it off, acting like Ray was just kidding. But the edge on Ray's voice—and the burning eyes and twitching jaw muscles—made it clear, Ray wasn't kidding at all!

"If you think I took it," said Lonnie, "then where is it? Where did I put it? I've been out on the floor with you. All the while. Check my locker if you want. But if you do," Lonnie added ominously, "you better find it. I don't like being called a thief. Especially not here in front of my friends."

The moment was tense. It could easily have gotten out of hand but, just then, Coach Dempsey came in.

"What's going on here?" the coach asked. No one said anything. The coach kept probing. Reluctantly Lonnie gave a quick summary.

"But I didn't touch his wallet," said Lonnie as he finished his report.

"I know you didn't, Lonnie," said the coach. "You know why I know? I have the wallet. When you guys were out doing warm-ups, I came back for my whistle. I saw this wallet on the bench. I've told you time and again not to leave valuables lying around the locker room. You are liable to lose them. Just as important," the coach said turning to Ray, "you can mess up a team. Worse yet, you can lose a friend. You fired too quickly, Ray. You were irresponsible with your money—and with your mouth. Here's your money. Now what are you going to do about your mouth?"

To Think About: Whew! Some speech! Okay, what should Ray do now? Can you list two things?

1. _____

2. _____

Prayer Thought: Ask God for help with protecting your neighbor's property and yours.

24
Teacher's Pet

Bible Reading: 1 Samuel 18:1 tells us about two good friends. Their names are _____ and _____ .

Anyone who asks Mrs. Ruther whether she has a pet student will be told, "I don't have pets. I treat all my students the same." But she doesn't.

There's no question that she wants, and tries, to treat everyone as equals. But it doesn't work out that way.

Ask any of the kids who Mrs. Ruther's favorite is and they will give the same answer: Marvin. When Mrs. Ruther can't hear, they call him *Marvelous Marvin,* imitating Mrs. Ruther's voice as they say it. He may be an ideal student to her but he is the pits as far as the rest of the class is concerned. No one likes him.

Marvin *is* a good student. He does his homework. But he also hangs around the front of the room all the time, waiting to do things for Mrs. Ruther.

"Let me empty the waste basket," Marvin will say. "I'll take the note to the office," Marvin will say. After school on rainy days Marvin will say, "I know where your umbrella is," and then goes and gets it. Marvin is a pain.

Lonnie didn't like Marvin much until the two of them had a conversation yesterday.

Lonnie and Marvin were standing in the hall waiting for the custodian to give them the overhead projector Mrs. Ruther wanted. Marvin had volunteered to get it for her. It was too heavy for one person. Lonnie had to be asked.

Out there in the hall, just standing around, Lonnie asked Marvin straight out, "Why are you always doing things for Mrs. Ruther? What are you after? The other kids think you want special favors from her. Why do you do that?"

"You really want to know, Lonnie?" asked Marvin. "I'll tell you. Mrs. Ruther wears the same perfume my mom did. She looks like her too. My mom died two years ago, just before we moved here. I miss her. I can't do anything for my mom anymore. I decided I'd be nice to Mrs. Ruther as a way of remembering my mom. If kids don't like how I act, that's tough."

Lonnie didn't believe Marvin really felt that unconcerned about the other kids in the class. Lonnie was sure Marvin wanted friends, but didn't know how to make them, especially feeling about Mrs. Ruther and his mom the way he did. Lonnie never told anyone what Marvin had said. He figured Marvin would do that when he was ready. But he made sure no one talked about *Marvelous Marvin* when he was around. And he decided to be Marvin's friend. Why not? Isn't telling private things the way friendships start and grow?

To Think About: Do friends in your school have serious concerns like Marvin's? What do you think? Read Matthew 11:28. If Lonnie had known that verse, would he have shared it with Marvin? How would Marvin have felt about it?

Prayer Thought: Ask God to help you be a friend to someone who needs one.

25
Laura Is Taller than Lonnie

Bible Reading: 1 Samuel 10:20–26 tells about how Saul became king. How was Saul different from the other men in the story?

Sometimes when Lonnie looked at Laura, he thought to himself, It's just not fair!

What wasn't fair? This: Laura was taller than Lonnie. Laura didn't think it was fair, either. She didn't like being tall. It made her feel like a big, gawky bean pole. She's taller than almost all the boys in her class. Only Freddy is as tall. Sometimes she stooped to hide her height.

Lonnie didn't picture Laura as big or gawky. In his eyes she was graceful and controlled. Not a bean pole, either. He'd even noticed that Laura was curvier than she used to be—and pleasantly so. But she was also taller than he by at least two inches. She appeared to be growing taller by the day! If only *he* were.

In his bedroom, on the wall near the door, Lonnie scratched a series of tiny marks. Each one is slightly above the other. They are almost invisible, hidden in the pattern of the wallpaper. But he knows they are there. He knows because every month he measures himself and makes a tiny mark. Once when he let the ruler on his head tilt too much, he thought he had shrunk! The differences, month to month, are disgustingly small. They are less than the width of the lead in his pencil some months.

If I were as tall as Laura, he thought, I'd be center on the team. And I'll bet I would high-jump over the four-foot bar.

Those are the kinds of thoughts Lonnie had. Once he imagined that he was tall enough to leap and touch the net on the basket. Another time he was tall enough to change the hands on the classroom clock without standing on a chair.

Sad to say, for the moment, Lonnie wasn't

as tall as Laura (like he wished). And Laura wasn't as short as Lonnie (as she wished). The truth is that each was about average for being a boy and girl their age. That meant Laura was the taller and Lonnie the shorter. Before long that would change. Probably.

To Think About: Is it always a burden to be smaller—or a blessing to be taller? Philippians 4:11 tells of a condition better than being either taller or shorter, being _____ with what life brings to you. (If you can't figure out the answer, go to the end of the next story.)

Prayer Thought: Ask God to continue blessing your growth, spiritually and physically.

26
The Way the Fight Began

Bible Reading: There is a *good* kind of fight. 1 Timothy 6:12 tells what it is.

Lonnie is no fighter. It's not that he can't fight. He can. But he doesn't like to. He might horse around with some of the guys. Lonnie doesn't mind that kind of fighting, but the real kind turns him off.

Vernon Edwards is no fighter either. Fighting isn't his style. Instead he starts fights. *That's* his style. Right now he is trying to get Mark to fight Lonnie. He started by telling Mark that if he was a real man, he'd make Lonnie kneel.

Lonnie laughed all that off at first. So did

Mark. In a way. But as the days went on, with Vernon pushing in the background, the laughing disappeared, and Lonnie and Mark's relationship got tense. When the kids were lined up for lunch, Vernon would shove Mark in front of Lonnie—and laugh. Mark let it happen. In time Mark did his own troublemaking. He would bump Lonnie in the hall. He'd act like it was an accident. But everyone knew differently.

Lonnie took the pushing around for a couple of days. Actually he couldn't think of a way to stop it. He tried to avoid Mark, ignore Mark, even laugh at the things Mark did. But Mark kept pressing him. Lonnie was beginning to feel trapped. Maybe that's why the next time Mark shoved him, Lonnie shoved back.

"That's it," said Mark. "I've had enough of you. When school's out I'll be waiting."

Uh-Oh. Now what?

To Think About: Ever been in a situation like Lonnie's? Any idea what Lonnie might do to avoid the fight?

Prayer Thought: Thank Jesus for standing by you in the good fight of faith.

27
Outside, After School

Bible Reading: Matthew 27:24–26 tells us about a man who tried to avoid blame. What is his name? ————————————

The afternoon was a blur to Lonnie. Finally the last bell rang. Mrs. Ruther dismissed the class. She sensed something going on and cornered Coach Piper for a little conversation. Would he mind keeping his eyes open after school? So, instead of going home right away, Coach Piper hung around and watched the students leave.

Vernon and Mark pushed their way out of school, racing to a corner between the school and Lonnie's home. A lot of the other boys hurried that way too. They didn't want to miss anything. When Lonnie turned down the street toward his home, he saw the gang waiting—15 or 20 boys. Mark was in front, and Vernon was smirking behind.

What to do? Lonnie weighed the situation. As he walked, he made up his mind. If it looked like there was going to be a fight, he would hit Mark as quickly, as hard, and as often, as he could. He wouldn't wait. The nearer he got to them the surer he was Mark wasn't going to back down. So he acted. Without a word he walked up to Mark and started flailing away.

Mark was stunned. Lonnie was supposed to be a pushover. Instead it was Mark who quickly found himself on the ground, covering his head with his arms. That's why he didn't see Coach Piper come up.

To Think About: People often do strange things when they are desperate. What do you think of Lonnie's desperate action?

Prayer Thought: Ask God to help you make the right decisions in tough situations.

28
An Odd Solution

Bible Reading: Psalm 133 tells how nice it is when people get along. How would you rewrite this short psalm to fit Lonnie and Mark?

"Easy does it," said Coach Piper as he unpiled Lonnie and Mark. "Do we have a misunderstanding here? Or, maybe you were just practicing some of the wrestling holds the high school wrestling team demonstrated in gym last week. That's it! Right? If this was a real fight, I'd have to take the whole pack of you to the principal. On the school ground, or off, it's a visit to the principal for anyone caught fighting, or encouraging fighting—even watching fighting. Anyone. But, of course, no one was fighting here. Right?"

All 20 guys ducked their heads, looked away, or mumbled a "no-fighting-here-Coach."

Knowing exactly what had been happening, the coach went on. "Vernon, as one of our school's big guys I'm guessing you were here to control this 'demonstration.' I know you wouldn't fight, allow a fight, or let someone get hurt, would you?"

Vernon nodded dumbly. The coach was right about one thing: Vernon wouldn't fight. Certainly not with Lonnie. Especially not now. He had no idea the kid was such a fearless buzz saw. Little did he know how scared Lonnie was!

Turning to Lonnie the coach continued, "You got a little carried away there, Lonnie. Why don't you help Mark up? Brush him off. Matter of fact you both can brush each other off. And maybe give a little handshake to make sure there are no hard feelings. If it were a fight, you couldn't do that, but since it's just a demonstration . . . ."

Lonnie and Mark did as the coach suggested. The events of the last few minutes had changed both of them. They had learned things about themselves, and about others, that they would never forget.

"Oh, by the way," said Coach Piper as he

turned to go, "I didn't realize how interested in exercise the rest of you are. Tomorrow in class I'll make sure you get a chance to *do* the exercise rather than watch it. Maybe a dozen laps around the track?"

All the guys groaned. Coach returned to school. Lonnie went home.

When Lonnie got older, he understood Coach Piper and his actions better. Coach Piper was like a policeman that day, bringing order and safety to a situation of confusion and threat.

To Think About: Can you think of a story in the Bible—or some verses from the Bible—that tell us about God's desire for order and safety in this world? If you can't, figure out whom you could ask for help in finding one. Write that person's name here: _____

Prayer Thought: Thank God for the people who show you how to get along.

29
It's a Small World

Bible Reading: Psalm 8 was written long ago by someone awed by the nature God created. Do you feel the same?

Listening to them talk, you would think that neither Lonnie nor Laura had ever been anywhere. Oh, yes, each had been to Chicago. Lonnie went to the museum with his aunt. Laura went to a Cubs game with her grandpa. (Both wished they had switched places!) But neither had been to a real far-away place—like Paris, or Disney World, or even Denver.

One Saturday afternoon in the early fall, just as the leaves were turning golden brown, Lonnie and Laura sat outside talking about places they had never been. They sat on the porch steps talking about school and kids and neighborhood news and places they would like to see.

Lonnie chose London and Greenland and Alaska. Laura's travel goals were Panama, Australia, and Israel. As they chattered about wonderful places around the world and the things they would like to see, Lonnie remembered something.

"Last week in science," he said, "Mrs. Dorn told us that every law of nature is observable in anyone's backyard. She said we don't have to go to Africa or Asia to see all the unusual things of the world. They are right here. I wonder if everything interesting about the world could be studied in our own neighborhood—without our ever leaving town?"

Whew! What a thought! Could it be possible to learn about the whole world, yet never leave the 200 block of Longridge? Is it possible that by studying the nine families who live on their block a person could learn truths about people—and places—all over the world? Wow!

Laura said, "You're something, Lonnie!

The things you pick up when no one thinks you are listening! What Mrs. Dorn said makes sense to me. If the Bible says that you can look at the heavens—the stars and the planets and all that stuff—and know things about God, I guess you could look around the earth and see things not only about God, but man too! Lonnie, you are a real thinker."

"I'm a what?" Lonnie asked with a laugh. "Careful what you call me!" He had to make a joke about it because he wasn't sure he understood what she had said. He wasn't even sure he understood what *he* had said.

To Think About: What do you think Lonnie's comment means? What could you learn about people around the world by studying your next door neighbor? And what *do* you learn about God by looking at the stars? Can you list just one thing? _____

Prayer Thought: Ask God to help you see the goodness of His creation in your own neighborhood.

30
The Millers Need Help

Bible Reading: How old do you think a person must be to get the treatment suggested in Leviticus 19:32? Put an age here: _____

Lonnie and Laura like the Millers. They think the Millers are nice. If you pressed them about what *being nice* means, they would say things like, "The Millers help us," or, "They listen when we come looking for help," or, "They always buy from us when we sell things." As nice as the Millers are, both Lonnie and Laura know something else about them that lots of people don't think is so nice, they are old.

How old? Some neighborhood kids say *very* old. At least 60. Lonnie's parents think old begins at maybe 70. But the Millers don't think of themselves as old. They feel quite young. They are only 74. But at 74, young as they feel, they do need help. They can't bend as easily as they used to. They can't work as long. Their doctor, and common sense, suggests some things they shouldn't do. Like wash windows. But who will do it for them? Whom should they ask? Guess.

It took the Millers a long time to develop enough courage to ask Laura and Lonnie to come talk with them. But one day they did. The four of them sat in the Miller's front room, drinking Coke and eating cookies. The conversation between them sputtered and dragged on, going nowhere, until Mr. Miller cleared his throat and made his move.

"Lonnie and Laura, Martha and I would like to ask you a question. Would you mind? We find we need some help. We want to know if either of you, or even both of you, would like a job. Like mowing the lawn in the summer and keeping up the yard? That's outside. On the inside we need windows washed and some cobwebs wiped away. It's hard for us to reach those webs," Mr. Miller said with a laugh, "and sometimes we can't even see them!"

Lonnie looked at Laura and Laura at Lonnie.

"We'll pay you, of course," said Mrs. Miller. "Seventy-five cents an hour!"

Lonnie thought, Is that all?

Laura said to herself, I hate washing windows.

The Millers sat waiting. They looked at Laura and Lonnie with sad little smiles playing at the edge of their mouths. Their eyes said, *Please?*

To Think About: Read the Leviticus verse again. Do you think God has any interest in what's going on in the Miller's front room?

Prayer Thought: Thank God for the older people He has placed in your life.

31
The Millers Get Some Answers

Bible Reading: In Genesis 18:22–33 God and Abraham negotiate. Who quit first? What does that say about God?

Lonnie sat frozen in his chair, looking at the Millers. He knew what he ought to say. So did Laura.

Laura spoke first. "I . . . I . . . I'd sure like to help. Really. But I'm not sure I'll have the time. School is getting harder and lots of weekends, after school too, I have cheerleading practice. Let me think about it. I'll ask the teacher whether it might be possible to skip some practices. But I'm not sure."

The way she said her *I'm-not-sure* told the Millers that Laura's *I'm-not-sure* meant *no-I-*

won't-do-it, no matter how many people she consulted.

Lonnie wasn't as delicate. "I'll do it, but 75 cents an hour isn't enough. There has to be more. I need to make some big bucks for Christmas."

"How much can you make doing other things?" asked Mr. Miller.

"Well, if I work for my uncle at his fruit stand, I make 10 or 11 bucks a Saturday. A paper route pays just as much. And when I work at the flea market, I sometimes get as much as $15.00 a day. Not always. But sometimes."

Mr. Miller paused and stroked his chin for a minute. "Sounds like I haven't been paying attention to the cost of labor. What if I up the pay to $1.50 an hour, with more if you do hard work, like windows? What do you say?"

"I say yes," said Lonnie.

"You're some negotiator," said Mr. Miller with a laugh.

To Think About: One thing God will not negotiate is His love for people. According to John 3:16 people are so important to Him that

He was willing to pay the highest price for them there could be. What was that price?

_____

Prayer Thought: Thank God for loving you enough to pay the highest price.

32
Down in the Dumps with Lee

Bible Reading: Luke 11:11–13 tells us that human fathers know how to do _____ things for their children. It also tells us that God acts in an even more loving way.

Lee wasn't actually crying. Not really. How could he be? He knew boys seven years old aren't supposed to cry. That's why, even though his head said he wasn't crying, his eyes didn't seem to know it. Laura heard Lee's quiet sobbing as she walked down the alley behind her house.

"Lee!" said Laura, "What's the matter? Are you hurt?"

Lee didn't look up. He didn't answer either. He just stayed slumped over beside his garage. His sadness was so thick Laura could feel it. Then, like a dam breaking, it all came flowing out. Tears. Hurt. Gloom. Sobs.

"Dad said he'd take me bowling today. But he hasn't come. Dad doesn't even want to live here anymore. I don't think he really loves me," Lee sobbed.

Laura listened. She didn't say a word until the speaking stopped and Lee's little body shuddered with the spent emotion of all that feeling.

"Oh, Lee!" Laura said quietly, "Don't worry. Your dad will come. Something must have happened. Maybe he had a flat tire. He'll be here soon. Or call. Just you wait. It will happen." She sat down beside him, put her arm around him, and big-sistered him.

It actually *was* only a few minutes before Lee's mother came out looking for him. She called his name, and both Lee and Laura answered. Following the sound of their response, she found the two sitting on the ground by the garage in the alley.

"Oh, there you are, Lee," his mom said. "Your dad just phoned. He had to go back to his office for an emergency, but he's on his way. He said he'll be here in a half hour or so. Did you hear, Lee? He's coming."

Lee smiled. First at his mom. Then at Laura. He was still smiling when his dad arrived.

To Think About: Laura could have just ignored Lee. Right? But she didn't. Do you think she sat down and talked with him because she was a Christian? Or because she was Laura? Or both?

Prayer Thought: Thank your heavenly Father for some of the good things He gives you.

33
Why Did I Ever Agree to Baby-sit?

Bible Reading: Psalm 51:10–12 tells us about someone whom God changed in an important way. What changes Laura in this story?

Laura didn't like washing windows. Not one bit. That's the reason she turned down the Miller's offer. She had tried washing windows only once. Once was quite enough. She didn't like the sponge's water leaking down her arms. Her back ached from all the reaching and stretching. And, no matter how she tried, there was always a spot she had missed. No window washing for her!

But baby-sitting! Now that was different. Especially if it was with the Humes twins. She just loved them. But she wasn't loving them at this very moment. At this very moment one was stuck behind a bedroom dresser that was too heavy for her to move. He couldn't get out no matter how hard he tried. His yowling scared her. The other was in the bathroom, locked in by his curious twitching of the bolt, and he was crying because he could neither unlock the door nor turn off the water.

Laura tried calling home for help. No answer. She searched the front yards for one of her friends. Nobody. She was about to call the police when she spied Mr. Miller out for an afternoon walk.

"Mr. Miller! Mr. Miller! Help me! Help me!" Laura yelled from the front door.

Mr. Miller's running days were over, but at her cry he set out on an old man's hustle. It didn't take him long to reach the doorway. Between Laura's breathless reciting of who was in peril where, and the bawling of the two boys, he formed a plan of action. First he went to the bedroom where he wedged the dresser out far enough for a frightened James Humes to escape.

Then using his little pocket knife, Mr. Miller snapped back the bathroom bolt saying, "Locked doors are no match for a sneaky old man like me!" Jason scrambled out of the bathroom as Laura dashed in to turn off the water. The tub was about to overflow!

Whew! What a relief! Laura had never known baby-sitting could be so unnerving. But then she hadn't ever before tried to handle Jason and James in one of their adventurous moods.

"Thanks, Mr. Miller," Laura sighed.

"Nothing to it," he said. Then he winked and added, "And what do you say we keep all this our little secret?"

Laura closed the door after him and took the twins out into the backyard. She sat relaxed in the swing as James and Jason played in the sandbox.

Maybe I *could* wash the Miller's windows, she thought.

To Think About: Mr. Miller sure rescued Laura. A great Christian truth is that God rescued us too. Do you know a six-letter, R-word for rescue? R _ _ _ _ _ (Check the end of the next story to see if you have figured it out.)

Prayer Thought: Recall a time when God rescued you. Thank Him.

34
Riding with Rick

Bible Reading: The writer of Psalm 46:1–3 could have added, "though the motorcycle rumble and sway!" The key thought is that _____is our help. Always. Right?

Lonnie didn't *need* to go to the high school that particular morning. As a matter of fact he was heading for Dockum Drugs, dollar in hand, ready for a candy splurge, when Rick Seeber pulled up next to him on his yellow Yamaha 250. What a motorcycle!

"Want a ride?" Rick asked. "I'm heading to school to pick up my football jersey. Want to come along for the ride?"

Would he! A ride with Rick! Wow! On the motorcycle! Double wow!

Rick handed Lonnie a safety helmet,

helped him adjust it, revved up the motor and told him to hang on. He said nothing about how dangerous a motorcycle can be. Nor did he warn Lonnie about all that could happen.

Thril-l-l-l-l! Lonnie had never been so excited in all his life. The speed of the bike, the noisy rumble of the motor, the soft bumpiness, the wind in his face. Best of all, it seemed like everyone he had ever known was on the street that day. Kids from school. Kids from the neighborhood. Kids from his soccer team. Kids. Kids. And more kids. He waved. He yelled. He grinned. He laughed out loud. Once, for just a few seconds, he even held up both hands over his head, all while flying down the street.

The trip to high school and back didn't take long. It wasn't that far. When they got back, Rick dropped Lonnie off in the alley that ran between their houses.

As Lonnie entered his house, higher than a kite, he discovered there was something faster than a motorcycle: the telephone. And there was something hotter than a Yamaha 250: his mom. She had heard about his ride. Already. Did she ever light into him!

Why are you so angry, Mom, Lonnie wondered as she lectured him. Why?

Had he listened more carefully, he would have heard words like *dangerous, scared, ask-me, who-do-you-think-you-are, worried,* and lots of others that really meant *"Please, don't grow up too quickly."* That's what they meant to his mom. To Lonnie they meant anger and confusion.

To Think About: Do you think Lonnie did something wrong? Figure out an answer and then ask your parents' opinion. Asking parents their opinion is one of the important purposes for which God gave them to us.

Prayer Thought: Ask God to help you and your parents hear the emotions behind the words you speak.

(The answer from story 34 is *redeem.*)

35
Michael Wynn Makes a Suggestion

Bible Reading: In Jonah 1:1–3 God tells Jonah to do something. Does Jonah obey Him? Does Lonnie obey in this story?

Lonnie saw a brown bag lying in the gutter down by Lincoln School. It looked too new and unused to be trash. He picked it up. It was heavy. It clanked. Opening the bag, he saw two empty beer cans. And two full ones. There were three funny-looking brown cigarettes too. At least that's what he thought they were. Not sure what to do, he tucked the bag under his arm and headed for home.

Michael Wynn was on his front porch that

Saturday morning, wondering what he would do with his day. Leaning against the front porch post, he noticed Lonnie coming up the walk with that bag under his arm.

"Hey, Michael, look what I've got," said Lonnie when he spotted his friend. And look Michael did.

"Do you know what this is?" Michael asked. "Marijuana! You better show this to your dad."

Lonnie gulped. If he hadn't talked to Michael, he might have done something super foolish. He had thought about popping open the beer and maybe taking a sip. And he'd even thought about lighting up one of those cigarettes. Just for fun. He'd had no idea they were marijuana!

"I'm glad you showed me what you found, Lonnie," his dad said later. "At the station we've heard there's been some funny stuff happening down by the school. Someone probably saw what looked like a police car, got scared, and dumped the bag out the car window. Nobody wants to get caught with this in their car! So I'm glad you came to me. And I'm glad Michael

106

suggested it. Let me take care of this from here."

To Think About: Christians often struggle with knowing what is "right." Did Lonnie do the "right" thing? How about Michael, did he?

Prayer Thought: Ask God to help you do the right thing, especially when it's tough.

36
Michael and Lonnie Talk

Bible Reading: Proverbs 1:10 is some great advice. Is there anything as effective when facing temptation as a very clear, *No?*

"How'd you know it was marijuana, Michael?" asked Lonnie. He had gone back to Michael's porch to report what happened.

"Just a guess, Lonnie," said Michael. He paused. "No, that's not really true."

"A cousin of mine got into trouble with drugs a couple of years ago," Michael continued. "He and two other kids were picked up after a party by the police. They had been smoking marijuana. One of the kids with him was put on probation because he was selling. The judge let my cousin off with just a warning.

Before he was caught, he showed me a marijuana cigarette. He even lit it up. The smell reminded me of sweaty people."

That surprised Lonnie. Smart and hardworking Michael knew about marijuana? Evidently. Lonnie was even more surprised as Michael continued talking. This time it was about beer.

"My aunt is an alcoholic. Recovered, now. When she was drinking, she told us she never drank anything stronger than beer. But she still was an alcoholic. I didn't know you could become an alcoholic by drinking beer. My aunt doesn't drink anymore. She's a member of Alcoholics Anonymous. But she's not quiet about it. She tells anyone who will listen what a problem drinking can be.

"And one thing more," Michael continued. "I think I know where that bag came from. Some guys from school were driving up and down Longridge last night. I saw them. They went down toward Lincoln School. Probably parked in the back. Last night about 10:30 I heard them racing this way. Someone, or something, scared them—like your dad said. I can't

109

prove it, but I'm sure they were the ones who had the stuff in their car." And still he talked.

"They used to ask me to go out with them. It didn't take me long to figure out what they were doing. I said no and stayed away from them. I decided a long time ago not to get involved with alcohol and drugs. How about you, Lonnie?"

To Think About: When some people use things that are harmful they argue, "I can do what I want. It's my life." Is that true? If you're not sure, check out 1 Corinthians 6:17–20.

Prayer Thought: Ask God for the strength to say no when you need to.

37
Saturdays Are Boring

Bible Reading: What dreams Joseph had! Read about them in Genesis 37:5–11. Did they cause him trouble? For an answer read verses 17–28 of that chapter.

Rake the leaves! Stack the lawn chairs! Wash the storm windows! Drain the lawn mower! Cover the rose bushes! All the stuff I have to do getting the house and yard ready for winter!

Those were the thoughts that whirled through Lonnie's brain as he grumped around the house and yard one Saturday morning. But, in between those griping thoughts his mind purred, in high gear, as he daydreamed about a time when he wouldn't have to do all this outside stuff!

When I'm grown up, I'm going to live in an apartment, he thought. No house or yard for me! I'll have an apartment in the city. And I'll belong to a country club like the Rolling Road Country Club. The club I join will have horses too. Then when I want to have fun I'll jump in my sports car and head out there. I'll be able to go there whenever I want.

As he stood leaning on the rake in the fall sunshine, thoughts piled on thoughts, and dreams on dreams. When I'm grown, I'll have a sailboat. I'll call it *The West Wind.* He crouched over as if he were at a tiller. His dream boat heeled over under the force of a 20-knot wind as he looked up at the billowing sail, spray blowing in his face. He could taste the salty brine!

After a few minutes a pinwheeling leaf dropping from a tree sent his imagination in another direction. When I'm grown, I'll have my own helicopter. No traffic jams for me. I'll paint it red and blue and dart from place to place. He twirled the rake over his head as if it were the rotor blade on his private copter.

Some leaves stirred a little at the force of his spinning. Just a few.

Suddenly Lonnie heard his mother calling from the back door. "Lonnie, are you out there? You better get busy. Dad left a list of things you are to do. He expects every last one done by the time he gets home. No messing around like last Saturday."

"Yes, Mom. I'll get them all done." And then as an afterthought, "What time is it?"

"A quarter past 10. Now get going!" answered his mom.

"10:15," he mumbled under his breath. "I thought it was almost noon. What a lousy way to spend the day! Cleaning. Raking. Washing. Boy, Saturdays are boring. Now, when I grow up . . ."

To Think About: Daydreaming is an important part of life. We practice many life skills in our daydreams. But sometimes daydreaming can cause problems. Can you think of any problems that daydreaming might cause you?

Prayer Thought: Thank God for the ability to dream.

38
Sunday Mornings Too

Bible Reading: What word in Psalm 122:1 expresses the writer's feelings about going to the house of the Lord? _____

Sunday was a sleep-in morning at the Grants. Mom usually stayed in bed later than on other days. Dad might, or might not, be up and gone before 8:00 A.M. Sometimes he had Sunday duty. And sometimes he rose early to putter around the yard. And sometimes he went golfing.

Betty was sure to sleep late. Eventually she would wander down the stairs, rubbing her eyes, wearing her awful, old fuzzy robe. It looked terrible but she liked it. For the first hour she was up she didn't talk except in short sentences.

"Where's the paper?" "I need milk." "You're in my seat." Betty was no fun that first hour Sunday morning.

Steve? The moment he came down he glued himself to the TV. Church services. Commercials. News. Cartoons. Not much else. Steve didn't care. Any TV was better than no TV.

Lonnie usually got up before anyone else. He'd get the paper from the front lawn, take it into the kitchen, spread it over the table, and fix himself some cold cereal. He'd read the funnies, waiting for the others to come downstairs, stretching as they came. Mom usually made pancakes or waffles. By that time Lonnie was ready for breakfast number 2. That early bowl of cereal kept him going until the good stuff was made. After the second breakfast he'd lie on the floor and check out the sports page.

Next door, at the Meyers, things were different. They were more organized. They had to be or they'd miss church. Lonnie could tell where the Meyers were in their routine by the noises they made: the garage door sliding up, voices of family members as they came outside, a closing car door, the revving of the engine, the slowly disappearing motor hum. Then silence. That silence meant the Meyers had left for church. Sunday school, too, Laura told him.

Lately Lonnie had a strange feeling as the Meyers left. He wished his family had someplace to go on Sunday mornings.

To Think About: What's the difference between Lonnie's Sunday morning and yours? Any way to make yours better?

Prayer Thought: Ask God to help you enjoy your worship time.

39
The
Thanksgiving Invitation

Bible Reading: Many Christians use Psalm 136:1 as their prayer after a meal. Does that make sense to you?

What will the kids and I do about Thanksgiving this year? thought Gerry Grant as she went about her housework. Their dad will be on duty all day, from dawn until nearly midnight, doing two shifts so some of the other policemen can have Thanksgiving Day off to be with their families. Of course, he'll get Christmas Day off that way. I guess that will be all right. We're not turkey eating people. No

117

one but Lonnie is really wild about it. Maybe I'll just get pizza for everyone and let it go at that. He likes that too.

Pizza for Thanksgiving? Maybe a nice, big, thick one with lots of cheese and pepperoni. As Gerry thought about her dinner plans, the phone rang. It was Doris Meyer from next door. She had heard Lonnie, Sr. was working on Thanksgiving Day and had suggested to her husband, "Let's invite the Grants to our house for Thanksgiving dinner."

"Good idea," he'd said. "Kristen and Betty get along. Laura, Lonnie, and Steven always seem to enjoy playing games with each other. I'm going to be glued to the TV set, watching football. That leaves you and Gerry talking together. Since you've gone back to work at the pharmacy, you don't have any chances to chat like you used to. And maybe Lonnie, Sr. could pull his squad car by for a while. Can't he do that on holidays, as long as he keeps his portable radio tuned in?"

And that's how the plans were made. The Grants and the Meyers agreed to have Thanksgiving together, except for Lonnie, Sr. Unless he could slip by.

After she hung up, Gerry Grant returned to her thinking. So much for pizza this Thanksgiving Day. Now let me see. I agreed to bring the dessert and the salad. I think I'll make a pecan pie *and* a pumpkin pie. And everyone likes cranberry salad. I'd better write down what I'll need.

To Think About: Both families are planning some parts of the Thanksgiving celebration. Do they seem to be forgetting the reason for celebrating the day?

Prayer Thought: Thank God for the foods you like best.

40
Thanksgiving Day

Bible Reading: There's a great story in 2 Kings 5:1–14 about a sick man and a little girl who spoke up to help him. First read about her in the Bible and then read this episode. What's the link between the two stories?

Thanksgiving Day events happened just as the two mothers planned. The Meyers and Grants had dinner together. Lonnie, Sr. pulled up in his squad car just as the turkey made it to the table. The Meyers had gone to church the night before. The Grants, as usual, hadn't quite made it. Actually, they hadn't really tried. Most of the Meyers had given up on inviting the Grants to go to church with them. *Most* of the Meyers. One hadn't given up at all: Laura.

She was still determined to find a way to get them there.

The turkey was great. Crispy brown and juicy. Even those who didn't really like turkey liked this one. And the stuffing! And the sweet potatoes! And the salads! And the pies! Everything was great.

The real fun started as soon as they were seated.

George Meyer said, "This meal needs a blessing! I'm not very good at fancy prayers. What do you say we use our normal prayer? But before we do that let's give everyone a chance to mention a couple things for which they are thankful. I'll begin. My list of things for which I am thankful include my neighbors and our country. There's more. But I'll stop with that."

Lonnie, Sr. plugged in, "Good friends and a great family." Gerry Grant mentioned health and a safe year. Doris Meyer added school and policemen. Betty and Kristen laughed as they listed rock music and clothes. Steve jumped in with Monopoly and Rocket, the dog. Lonnie was having trouble coming up with something that hadn't been mentioned until he thought of his rising math grades and Michael Wynn. Then came Laura.

Laura said, with a gulp, "I'm thankful for our church and another chance to invite the Grants to go there with us for Christmas."

There was a long pause. Mr. Meyer started to say something to cover over Laura's comments, but Mrs. Grant broke in first.

"Your invitation is all we needed, Laura," Mrs. Grant said. "This year my husband is off on Christmas. We'll go with you."

And that's how Laura got the Grants to go to church.

To Think About: Laura, like the Holy Spirit, didn't give up. As a matter of fact, the Holy Spirit used Laura to work in the lives of her neighbors. Do you know anyone the Holy Spirit can work in through you?

Prayer Thought: Ask the Holy Spirit to help you share your faith with a friend.

41

A as in Advent

Bible Reading: Zechariah 9:9 tells us that a
_____is coming. His name is
J__s__s.

Steven brought it home from the Meyers. It was a special kind of calendar, they said. The days' numbers were printed on little paper doors which, when opened, revealed an angel, or a shepherd, or a Christmasy picture.

"Hey, Mom," yelled Steven as he came through the back door, "Look what I've got. It's an *admit* calendar. Kristen Meyer gave it to me. She says she gives them to friends every year."

Mrs. Grant checked out the doors and peeked at one of two of the pictures. In the process she noticed the colorful title: Advent Calendar.

"Very good, Steven. You have it almost right. But it's not an *admit* calendar. It's an *Advent* calendar," said Mrs. Grant. Even as she spoke, she was afraid of his next question. Afraid or not, out it popped.

"Advent calendar? What's an Advent calendar?" asked Steven. "I've never heard of an Advent calendar. Have I?"

"I don't think you have, Honey. But I remember Mrs. Meyer talking about it one time. I think she said that Advent is the period of time just before Christmas. Some Christians use these calendars as a kind of countdown, like when we shoot rockets into space. Advent has something to do with getting people ready for Christmas. I see you've got a little book too. Look, a story for every day 'til Christmas. How about reading the book together this year? And you can open a door each day."

"Oh, yes," said Steven, "I'd like that."

And they did. Each day. By the time they got to December 24, Steve and his mom knew a lot about Advent. Christmas too. They discovered that the word *Advent* means *He is coming*. Whom do you think the *He* is?

To Think About: What do you know about Advent? If you wanted to learn more, where would you look? See if you can find out what an Advent wreath is.

Prayer Thought: Thank God for the gift of His Son.

42

The Reason for the Season

Bible Reading: God sent His _____.
That's what Galatians 4:4–5 says. But for what
purpose?

Laura liked her pin. It wasn't very large,
but it was bright. Lots of people looked at her
pin with its pretty holly wreath edging and the
words, *Jesus is the Reason for the Season.* That's
what it said!

Mrs. Ludwig gave all the kids pins in Sunday school. The boys took theirs home for their
moms. As Mrs. Ludwig handed out the pins,
she explained the gift.

"You've been a wonderful class. Really. I
don't know when I've had more fun teaching
than this year. I decided I wanted to express

my pleasure in you and also give you something that might help you share your faith. I chose this little pin. It has helped me talk about Jesus. It doesn't force my faith on other people. I just wear it. When someone asks me what the pin means, I accept their question at face value and as a signal to speak the truth."

"You mean you tell them about Jesus? Just like that?" asked Jodi. "You use the pin to talk?"

"I sure do," answered Mrs. Ludwig. "I tell them there would be no Christmas without Jesus. I tell them that Santa is nice, and carols are pretty, and trees are beautiful. And I assure them that presents are great. But I also tell them that at the heart of it all is Jesus Christ. And then I say something like, 'You know there are people who don't realize that Jesus, and what He did for me, is the reason we have Christmas.' I sometimes even talk to them about sin and how our Savior, Jesus Christ, came so He could take upon Himself all the sin we commit. Then I say John 3:16.

"See how simple it is? It all starts with this pin. Maybe you will have the chance to say many of the same things when people ask you about it. Or if they ask about your Christmas tree. Or why you go to church. Be ready for chances to witness. Then, when a chance comes, the Holy Spirit will help you to be bold."

That's what Mrs. Ludwig told the class.

To Think About: Do you know John 3:16? Fill in the words without looking. If you miss some, look it up. "For _____ so _____ the _____ that He gave His only begotten _____ that whoever _____ in Him would not _____ but have everlasting _____ .

Prayer Thought: Ask the Holy Spirit to help you witness your faith to a friend or family member.

43
Deck the Halls

Bible Reading: People like to be with people, especially in their learning times. John 21:1–17 makes that clear.

The Meyers said Laura could invite friends over to start decorating for Christmas. She invited Ted and Lou and Karen from the neighborhood, and Lonnie of course.

They all came at the same time. Lots of noise. Lots of faces shiny red from the cold. Laura's mom had started the popcorn, and her dad promised cider later. He said he'd heat it up and put a cinnamon stick in it. Yummy. But first they had to decorate the tree.

"Okay now, Laura, where do we start?" asked Lonnie. "Your dad has the tree set up where he wants it. So how about starting with the little soldiers and then the bird ornaments and the garlands and then the . . . ."

"Whoa. Wait a minute. Hold up," said Laura. "I need to explain some things. I decided that I'd like to try making a *Christian* Christmas tree this year. This article I cut out tells how to do it. The evergreen tree reminds us that our life in Christ is always alive (and so is He) even in the toughest times. See how it works? Then we'll make 33 roses and put them on the tree because . . . ."

"I know why," said Lou. "Because Jesus lived 33 years on earth. Right?"

Laura nodded.

"How did you know that, Lou?" Lonnie asked.

"Not all of us lie around the house on Sunday morning, Lonnie. I go to Sunday school. I learned Christ's age years ago. You'd know it too—if you went. You'd find out a lot of other things that could surprise you."

Lonnie said nothing.

Laura continued, "Then I thought we might put on gold, red, and blue ornaments to remind us of the gifts brought to Jesus. And we'll put on only white lights, to look like stars. Way up on top I want to place one big star like the one that guided the Wise Men to Jesus. And we'll put a crèche under the tree."

"A what?" asked Lonnie.

Laura looked at him. "A manger scene, Lonnie. With Mary and Joseph and baby Jesus and some animals and shepherds, all in a little stable."

"Well, why didn't you say so?" said Lonnie. "Boy, I thought I was going to decorate a Christmas tree and here I am in the middle of a religion class. Well, better late than never. Let's get going. But first, pass the Christian popcorn. It *is* Christian, isn't it? Everything else around here is." Lonnie was laughing as he said it, but his eyes had a serious glint.

To Think About: Have you ever heard of a Christian Christmas Tree? Would you like to make one? How would you decorate it?

Prayer Thought: Thank Jesus for giving you the gift of everlasting life.

44
Let's Go Caroling

Bible Reading: According to Job 38:7 what "sings together"?

_____

_____

So why shouldn't we?

When Mr. Grant opened the door, he could hardly believe his eyes. Standing there on his porch were the Wynns and the Millers and the Meyers, smiling and bundled up against the cold. He heard what sounded like a harmonica note, and then the whole bunch broke into song.

"Joy to the world, the Lord is come . . . ." The Grants were being caroled. When that song was done, the carolers sang: *O Little Town of Bethlehem.*

"Come on in," welcomed Mr. Grant. "Come on in. I haven't been caroled since I was a kid. You sound great!"

It was cold. He didn't have to ask twice. They all pushed in. Lonnie, Sr. kept on complimenting them until Mr. Miller said, "Well, if you liked it so much, why don't you and the family come with us? We're going around the block and ending up at our house for hot chocolate and cookies."

Lonnie, Sr. looked at Gerry. Gerry looked at him. They didn't have to look at Steven. He already had his coat on. He was bringing Betty's too. Lonnie didn't need any encouragement. He knew when there was going to be fun. A little struggling into coats, some advice about singing la-la-la whenever you forget words, and away they went.

In many ways it was a strange sort of evening. It was so warm out in the cold! Everyone felt safe and secure, even in the darkness. The carolers were welcomed everywhere. By everyone. And at every house, the people for whom they sang put on their coats and came along too. Mrs. Baker (and Lee) were the last they visited on their block. Cold as it was, the group made a couple of extra stops across the street so the two of them could carol too. Then everyone squeezed into the Miller's home.

Lonnie and Laura looked at each other knowingly when Mrs. Grant, peering out the Miller's window to see if anyone had been left outside, said, "Martha, you have the cleanest windows I've ever seen. I wish I could get mine this sparkling. Who helps you?"

Martha Miller smiled, winked at Lonnie and Laura, and said, "Oh, I have some special helpers."

To Think About: A closeness develops when people have a common purpose and support each other in it. 1 John 4:7–11 tells us that for Christians the name of that closeness is _____. It doesn't come from caroling. It comes from _____.

Prayer Thought: Thank God for a good time you have had with Christian friends.

45
Lonnie Goes Shopping

Bible Reading: What could Proverbs 18:16 mean? Is there any Christmas application of those words?

It was the second Saturday in December, and Lonnie was concentrating on buying Christmas presents. He had been surprised at how much money he had made from working for his uncle and for Mr. Miller. Now the money-saving days were over. It was time to spend, spend, spend. He was out buying gifts.

At the top on his list were gifts for his mom and dad. Then came Betty and Steven. And something for the guy whose name he had drawn at school. He hardly knew him. But it didn't matter. The gift limit was one dollar. Not much choice for a buck!

Way back in his mind Lonnie was worrying about something else. He couldn't make up his mind whether he ought to buy Laura a present. She had asked him what he wanted for Christmas. Did that mean she was just asking, or was she trying to get an idea of what she could get for him? In some ways he was hoping she would get him a gift. In other ways not. If she bought one, so would he. But was she? It was all very confusing. He'd never bought a gift for Laura or any girl before. He wasn't sure what to do. Maybe he should ask Betty what she thought. Yes, that's a good idea. Ask Betty. Now back to Mom and Dad. What could he get?

To Think About: Lonnie was sure having a hard time figuring out what to do. Why do you think he was having so much difficulty? Would it have made any difference if Lonnie had thought about Christmas as a Christian event? What's your opinion?

Prayer Thought: Ask God's help in thinking up some "free" gifts that can be given to your family any day.

46
A Christmas Eve Invitation

Bible Reading: John 3:1–17 tells the story of Jesus' response to N—c—d—m—s. I wonder how many times he had come to Jesus after dark before this wonderful conversation took place?

Remember the Thanksgiving dinner at the Meyers? Remember how they invited the Grants to their meal? Well, a letter arrived at the Meyer home the second week in December. The letter read:

The Grant Family of Longridge Avenue herewith invites the Meyer family of Longridge Avenue to Christmas Dinner at 11:00 A.M. on Christmas Day.

R.S.V.P. Regrets Only.

The outside of the envelope was decorated with little snowmen and Christmas seals. The address was carefully printed and decorated with old fashioned flourishes.

"R.S.V.P. Regrets Only," Laura read aloud. "Whatever does that mean?"

"You don't know?" teased Kristen. "I thought you knew everything. It means you don't have to respond to the invitation unless you aren't coming."

"Now, girls. Be nice. Remember the season. This is the gentle time of year," said their mother.

After those few words she went on, "I wonder if we ought not only accept their invitation, but invite them to come over for some cookies and punch on Christmas Eve? They know we go to church. Maybe we could ask them to make it 9:00 P.M. or so after we get back. I'll just drop over and see. No use writing this all out. We don't need all this formality between us," she laughed.

A few minutes later Doris Meyer was in the Grant kitchen drinking coffee with Gerry.

"What a lovely invitation you sent! And so

beautifully done," Mrs. Meyer said. "We're thrilled to come on Christmas and we'd like you to come over for cookies and punch on Christmas Eve, around 9:00 P.M., if that fits your plans."

"Actually, it fits right in," said Gerry. "Lonnie, Sr. is off-duty on Christmas Eve and Christmas Day. We thought we'd go to church, *your* church, on Christmas Eve. Lonnie, Jr. has been hinting around about it. Betty thinks it's a good idea. And you know Steven, he'll go where we all go. Do you mind if we tag along that evening? And then come to your house afterwards?"

Mind? Mrs. Meyers couldn't believe her ears. She was delighted.

To Think About: A Thanksgiving dinner leads to a Christmas invitation that sets the stage for Christmas Eve worship! That's something! Could the Holy Spirit be at work in there somewhere? What do you think?

Prayer Thought: Thank God for the times you can see His Spirit at work in your life.

47

The Christmas Eve Service

Bible Reading: The pastor read Luke 2:1–7 the night Lonnie went to church. Read it yourself. Would Lonnie have trouble understanding any of the words?

As far as Laura was concerned, Christ Church was beautiful beyond description on Christmas Eve. But, then, her opinion shouldn't be surprising. She believed it was beautiful all the time. She loved the padded oak pews. She gazed in awe at the marble altar with the carving of the Lord's Supper just above it. The windows, the wide center aisle, the candles, she liked them all. But what made Christmas Eve the nicest were the lowered lights. And the many flickering candles. And the Christmas tree. It was like the one at the Meyer's home. It, too, had 33 roses and white twinkling lights. But it was bigger. Much bigger.

Even though the service wouldn't start for 15 minutes, the church was nicely filled by the time the Meyers and Grants arrived. The parents found seats together, with Steven wedged in between his mom and dad. Lonnie, Laura, Betty, and Kristen sat two rows farther up.

Looking through the service folder, Betty whispered to Kristen that she knew all the hymns. Laura checked out the listing of things to come. Lonnie just leaned back and let the moment fill him. The organ music flowed over him. He felt like he was in a holy place, warm and secure, and it was pleasant and so quiet.

Then the mood changed. The organist began playing more vigorously.

What's going on? Lonnie wondered. He looked at his bulletin. It was time for the first hymn. Everyone around him stood up, just like the bulletin asked them to. Then the organ really got loud and everyone began to sing.

When the congregation hit that first note, Lonnie was startled. "Joy to the world," rolled out with enthusiasm. The man behind him let loose with more enthusiasm than accuracy. But that was okay. The three girls surprised him with the sweetness of their singing and their sound of shiny sincerity. The first thing he knew, Lonnie went into action, too, a little quietly at first. But by the time congregation got to, "Let heav'n and nature sing . . . ," everyone, Lonnie included, was doing just that.

The next 40 minutes, including the sermon, passed with agreeable speed. Before he knew it, Lonnie was standing in the aisle, packed among people, inching his way to the doors. He could hardly wait to get outside. He had questions to ask. Did he ever have questions!

To Think About: What questions might Lonnie have after his first visit at church? Write down one or two:

_____

_____

Prayer Thought: Thank God for the things you enjoy most about your church.

48
Lonnie Asks Questions

Bible Reading: Read Titus 3:1–7. Why would these verses make a good Christmas Eve Scripture reading?

As you might have guessed, Steven was asleep by the time the service ended. Mr. Grant carried him out and teased Pastor Hinz about putting the boy to sleep. The pastor laughed, though he'd heard that line before. Outside in the chill the two families quickly agreed that Kristen and Betty would ride home with the Grants (and sleeping Steven), while Laura and Lonnie would ride in the Meyer's car.

"What was the wreath thing with the candles?" asked Lonnie, even before the car heater could warm up enough to make things comfortable.

"You mean the Advent wreath?" answered Laura. "You remember Advent—the four weeks before Christmas when we get ready for Christ's coming? We light one more candle each Sunday during Advent. On Christmas Eve we light the candle in the middle. It's the Christ candle. Lighting the last one means Christmas is here."

"Okay," Lonnie nodded. "Now let me ask something else. Why did the pastor talk so much about sin in his sermon? I thought Christmas was a happy time. Why did he keep talking about mistakes?"

Mrs. Meyer moved in on that one. She wanted to be sure that the conversation didn't end with Lonnie having all the questions and Laura knowing all the answers.

"Lonnie, you picked up on that real quick!" Mrs. Meyer said. "Many people don't even notice that pastors talk about sin on Christmas Eve. You are sharp." Lonnie beamed.

"In one sense," Mrs. Meyer continued, "sin

is the main subject of Christmas. Because of it, Christ had to come! The word *sin* means to make a mistake, or miss a target, or refuse to obey. Those are the things that get us into trouble with each other and separate us from God. The Bible says that. Sin, whether intentional or unintentional, is very destructive. And everyone sins. All the time."

Lonnie frowned. He wasn't sure he understood that. He had thought sin was only doing something bad, breaking a rule. This was getting deep. Mrs. Meyer sensed his growing confusion. She decided to change the approach a little.

"Do you know how sin came into the world?" she asked.

To Think About: We'll wait for Mrs. Meyer's explanation. While we are, go back to her definition of sin. Can you find a picture or a story in a newspaper that illustrates the world's sinfulness?

Prayer Thought: Confess a sin that you have committed today and thank God for His forgiveness.

49

What about the Garden, and Sin?

Bible Reading: Genesis 3:1–7 is a "bad-news" story in the Bible. Read it and see if you agree.

It began snowing hard as the car left the church. Mr. Meyer didn't drive very fast. The roads were slippery and uncertain. But going slow was all right with Mrs. Meyer. It gave her plenty of time to talk about God's plan without hurrying.

"In the beginning God made everything perfect," Mrs. Meyer explained. "At each day's end, as another part of His work was finished, God would say, 'That's good.' When everything

146

was finished, His world was perfect. He wanted it that way.

"Then sin came," she continued. "Uninvited. You know—like when someone slips into the backyard where you and your friends are playing and starts trouble. We believe that the one who brought sin is Satan, the devil. He did it by testing Adam and Eve. Eve failed his challenge and did what she wasn't supposed to do. On top of that she encouraged Adam to sin as well. Adam and Eve disobeyed God. In their disobeying, sin came into the world. Sad to say, it came to stay. People have disobeyed ever since.

"Like right there," said Mrs. Meyer excitedly, pointing to a speeding car. "Did you see that? That car ran right through the red light! We could have been killed! Doesn't that guy know its snowing? Did he make a mistake? Or did he refuse to obey? No matter. If Mr. Meyer hadn't been driving so carefully, it wouldn't have made any difference. He would have hit us. Whew! Well, let me think, that's the way it is with sin. It can and does do terrible damage, regardless of the reason.

"After Adam and Eve sinned, God came looking for them. But He did not reject them. As a matter of fact, He gave them good clothes and the promise of a Savior. Adam and Eve left the garden where things had been perfect and entered the world, the sinful world.

"It was that world full of sin that Christ was sent to gain back. Each Christmas we recall the reason the Christ Child was sent. He came because of sin all around us, and sin within us. God had to help. And He did."

To Think About: The story of Christmas begins in the Garden of Eden. Circle the answer: T F

Prayer Thought: Ask God to help you remember the connection between creation and Christmas.

50
And the Promise

Bible Reading: John 3:16 is so direct and clear! It tells us that God loves us and saved us. Count the words in the verse. Put their total here: _____.

Well, if the sin Mrs. Meyer talked about makes sense to you, it didn't make a lot of sense to Lonnie. Maybe it was because while he was listening to Mrs. Meyer, he was also nervously watching the road. The weather was bad, and the streets were slippery.

"I wonder if we aren't talking too much about the dark side of Christmas," said Mr. Meyer. "I mean about sin and Satan. That's basic background stuff, but it isn't the whole of our celebration. Our larger accent is on the *promise* God made. And the promise God *kept!* I'm out here driving through all this snow on this wintry night because I'm celebrating God and the promise He made."

"I like that part better too," said his wife. "I've talked enough. Tell us about the promise, George." And he did.

"At the beginning, when sin entered the world, things turned bad between Adam and Eve; and between Adam, Eve, and God. Adam and Eve hid from God; they blamed each other and Satan for what had happened. Into that sorry mix of hiding and blaming, God introduced a ray of light, a promise. He said He would provide a way to correct the destruction of sin. It wasn't an easy solution. But it was a solution." The snow had almost stopped. The trees, the streets, the houses—everything—was covered with a layer of white. Against the whiteness, street lights sparkled as if they were crystal. The neighborhood looked beautiful and inviting, like a Christmas card's Christmas Eve.

"Oh, Daddy," said Laura, "I love to hear about the promise. Can I tell that part?"

Without waiting for an answer she continued, "Right away, Lonnie, after Adam and Eve sinned, God made that promise Daddy mentioned. His promise was that He would defeat Satan, and Satan's power over Adam and Eve. That was His promise. Actually, the rest of the Bible is the story of how God has been faithful to His promise. He never changed. Through Jesus He beat Satan and put His children in the garden again. Only the name of the garden has been changed. It's no longer called Eden. It's called heaven!"

Laura never even slowed down. She kept on talking. "Jesus is God's promise fulfilled. When Jesus was born, it was the end for Satan and a new beginning for the rest of us. God kept His word. He saved us through Jesus. That's what the angels told the shepherds in the fields of Bethlehem. Remember?"

To Think About: What six letter word in Luke 2:11 did the angels call God's Promised One? Write it here:

_____

Prayer Thought: Use words from one of your favorite Christmas carols to thank God for saving you.

51
A New/Old Family Tradition

Bible Reading: Psalm 150 lists a whole lot of ways to give thanks. How many do you count? _____ How many of these could you do today? _____

The two family-filled cars pulled into their separate driveways about the same time. There was a lot of running back and forth between the houses as everyone got into more comfortable clothes.

All the motion was all right with Doris Meyer. It gave her a chance to get the cookies and hot chocolate ready. Actually, she had planned to serve a lot more than cookies and a hot drink. There were cheeses, nuts, and dips. There were crisps and cakes and special sweets.

There was punch and cider and coffee. *And* hot chocolate. There were icing-santas and cute little candy wreaths. There was enough great food to wake up Steve!

The Meyers and Grants loaded their plates from the buffet, then moved into the family room to sit around the tree near the fire. Mr. Meyer put Christmas music on the stereo.

"I like your Christmas Eve family tradition of going to church," said Lonnie, Sr. to George Meyer. "I think I'll do whatever I can to make sure I'm off duty every Christmas Eve from now on. With my years of service on the police force I ought to be able to arrange that. As I've sat here, one of my childhood family Christmas traditions came to mind. I haven't thought about it in years. Sometime over the Christmas holidays we would gather around the Christmas tree. Each person gave everyone a wish gift. We'd wish something for other family members. I always had trouble thinking of what to wish. Tonight I have no trouble. I wish the whole Meyer family another year of peace in their house and 365 more days next door to us."

"What a great tradition!" Mr. Meyer said. "And what a great wish. Until I have a chance to think about it more, Doris and I wish you the same. We'd wish you better neighbors, but we're staying," he added with a twinkle in his eye.

"I'm not ready to send a wish tonight," Betty said. "But that's a great tradition you remembered, Dad. You've never mentioned it before. Can we save it for next year? We'll all have 365 days to get ready."

A lot of great things are going to happen between now and next Christmas, Lonnie thought. I'll know what to wish for everyone. He looked around and said, "Sure. Let's do it. And let's do it your way, Betty. Next Christmas."

And that's how a Grant tradition was reborn.

To Think About: What is God's Christmas wish for all His children?

Prayer Thought: Thank God for some of the blessings you have received since last Christmas.

52
It Begins to Fall into Place

Bible Reading: Ecclesiastes 3:1–2 says there is a _____ for everything. Is there even a time for understanding to grow?

The snow stopped just after midnight. That's about when the Grants crunched their way to their house. Dad carried sleeping Steve into the house and up to bed. Mom went along to tuck Steven in.

Betty yawned her good night and headed for bed. That left Lonnie to check the lights and lock the front door before he climbed the stairs. Too big a job? Not for him. He was getting to be a man, so he ought to do the grown-up tasks.

As Lonnie opened his bedroom door, the

window beckoned to him. He didn't turn on his lamp. Guided by the outside shimmer, he found his way to look out on his world. Almost all the houses were dark. The street lights reflected brightly off the snow. The Dockum Drug neon sign flashed on and on, Christmas Eve or not. A few cars whispered through the streets on the cushion of snow. All was calm. All was bright. Just like the carol said.

His cheek against the window, Lonnie thought of the day, the fun with the Meyers, of the many things he had seen and heard. Last year on Christmas Eve he had just jumped into bed and gone to sleep.

As tired as he was, Lonnie found himself trying to put the day's experiences together. The Christmas Eve service and the conversations in the car. He was beginning to have some feelings about this Christian stuff. If you understood a little about sin, and the garden, and something about God's promises, then Christmas was very different from the Rudolph and Santa and ho-ho-ho he had always experienced before.

Enough of that tonight. Better get to bed. Tomorrow there would be presents to open.

To Think About: Have you noticed any "thinking" changes in your life? Does God draw you closer to Him as you get older? How? Isn't that what's happening to Lonnie?

Prayer Thought: Thank God for the growing understanding He is giving you.

53
Lonnie Makes a Decision

Bible Reading: Nicodemus made a decision. John 3:1–2 tells us he decided to visit _____, but he did so at night.

Christmas came and went. It had been a great one for Lonnie. Laura felt the same way. Each had gotten more gifts than they expected. Lonnie and Laura had both received the usual Christmas games. But this year clothes were what they liked most. And both got lots. Lonnie even found a little bottle of after-shave lotion in his stocking. The tag read: From Santa.

Lonnie didn't give Laura a Christmas present. He decided he'd wait and maybe give her a birthday present instead. Her birthday was coming up soon. He didn't realize her birthday

158

was on a day called Epiphany. All he knew was that there would be a party for her January 6.

But something else happened this Christmas. Lonnie had made a decision.

"Mom," he'd said, "starting next week I'd like to go to church. I'd even like to try Sunday school. I could ride with the Meyers. But couldn't we go as a family?"

Lonnie's mom wasn't totally surprised by the request. She'd had that church-going feeling too. Was this their moment to act, she wondered?

"Let me talk to your dad about this," Mrs. Grant answered. "I think we all might want to go to church a little more. But we'll need to make arrangements."

It wasn't until after he had talked with his mom that Lonnie told Laura of his decision. He was laid back about his explanation.

"I figure if I can learn as much as I did riding home from church on a snowy night, I could *really* learn if I got serious about it!" Lonnie laughed.

So that's how it happened. Lonnie's life took a zig. Or was it a zag? Anyway, things changed. After that decision a lot of other things began to change for Lonnie and Laura too. Was it because Lonnie wanted to go to church? Or was it because Lonnie and Laura were growing in so many ways? Or maybe, some of both?

To Think About: Psalm 51:10 tells who changed Lonnie, and how it happened. In your own words complete this sentence: Lonnie changed when ———————————— gave him a ———————————— ————————————.

Prayer Thought: Ask God to continue to bless you each day as you grow in Him.